Sugar and Spice and *All Those Lies*

Between Two Worlds: Book 4

Evy Journey

Sojourner Books
Berkeley, California

Sugar and Spice and All Those Lies/ Evy Journey. – 2nd ed.
ISBN 978-0-9962474-4-3

Book Layout ©2013 BookDesignTemplates.com
Book Cover Design: www.tugboatdesign.net
Manuscript reviewer: David King
Copy Editor: Julie Mianecki

Poets have been mysteriously silent on the subject of cheese.
Gilbert K. Chesterton

Cooking is like love. It should be entered into with abandon or not at all.
Harriet van Horne

I cook with wine, sometimes I even add it to the food.
W.C. Fields

There is a communion of more than our bodies when bread is broken and wine drunk.
M.F.K. Fisher

Content: Sugar and Spice and All Those Lies

Prologue

I'm alive. I'm dead. I'm in-between. In that limbo where my vital signs hover just above death. I rise above my body and look down on it, lying on a gurney. Hospital staff are rushing me along the brightly-lit hallway to the operating room. One of them holds an oxygen mask on my face. Another, a bag of intravenous fluid connected to my veins by a tube.

I'm not ready to die yet. These good people anxious to rescue me don't know that my resolve is the only thing that is keeping me alive. No, I'm not ready to die— I've only just begun to live. I have yet to prove to myself, to the world, that I have what it takes to prevail.

My family—now on their way to the hospital— doesn't know yet what happened to me. And except for one detective, neither do the police. I see him now by the foot of the gurney, keeping pace with the nurses. He's scowling, his lips pressed into a grim line.

A tall, taut, and solitary man, he has deep-set gray eyes clouded by too many images of violent death and a mouth that hangs perpetually open in disgust or despair. So much darkness he has already seen in his thirty odd years in this world. He needs to piece together the facts that constitute the attempt on my life, events that may have led to it, and various fragments of my past to understand what brought me to this point.

The first time I met him, I fell in love with him. There was something primal about him, some paternal, animalistic instinct to save hurt or fallen victims. Like me, maybe. It gave him power and it made him irresistible to me.

But fate is fickle. It teases. It entices. One day, something quite ordinary happens to you. Yet, you sense that that ordinary something can change your life. Not necessarily for something better, but for something new. Fate is dangling before you the promise of a world that, before then, was totally out of your reach. How can you not seize it?

Now, of course, I see the end of that promise. And it's not where I want to be.

It's tragic, don't you think, that the end of that promise should be right here on a gurney, with me fighting for my life? It certainly is not what I hoped for.

How could it end this way? I embraced life, took chances, but half-dead on this gurney, I wonder: Am I paying with my life? But, like I said. I'm not ready to die yet.

Chapter One

Du Cœur

Sous chef Guy watches to my left, his hands clasped behind his back. He's tense, struggling not to reach for the bowl of crumbled nori on the counter to my right. The part-adult, part-adolescent strawberry blond with a pointed chin—bright eyes darting between me and Guy—watches from behind us, waiting to be handed two plates of the course I'm preparing to garnish.

I take a pinch of the nori, sprinkle it over raw tuna on one plate. Another pinch over the tuna on the second plate. I look up at Guy.

Hands finally unclasped off his broad back, he picks up one plate, thrusts it to me. "Okay Gina, your turn. Take this to table 29."

My mouth opens to protest. Just as quickly, I close it again. I've learned the ritual, but this is the first time I'll be participating in it. I'm frazzled enough and going out to the dining room will make me jumpier.

Guy hands the second plate to the strawberry blond. He's only been serving a few weeks. His bright eyes, even brighter smile, the spring in his steps still reek of his gratitude for being lucky enough to work at Du Cœur.

On each of the large plates, the two ounces of red tuna seem to float on a wide expanse of white porcelain. I still don't get why our plates have to be ten times the size of the portions we serve. Well, maybe, not ten times. Extravagantly large, anyway.

Strawberry blond follows me out of the bustling brightly-lit kitchen. Laure, the owner and chef de cuisine, thinks all her cooks should occasionally go out to the dining room and serve customers. I'm not quite sure why. Something to do with the buzz between cook and customer when creator and consumer meet. Plus comments you may get can tell you a lot about what customers like (or don't like) about your dish—these, I admit, might sometimes hurt, but they'll be useful.

The original idea for the dish I'm serving is mine. Guy played with it and we all taste-tested the many variations he and I came up with until we found the combination that made our taste buds sing.

But a new dish isn't ready until Laure says so. She tastes it, squints at it for presentation and color and when you see her smile and wink at you, you know it's a go. If not, you try again. She's easy, though. Many times, she herself tweaks the dish a little, before she rewards you with that wink and recites her culinary mantra:

Dining isn't just about flavors; it's also textures, color, and context. Context to her is anything from the layering of flavors to the ambiance in the dining room.

Before I can walk into the dining room, Marcia, the easy-going pastry chef who's become my best friend, steps away from her station, whispers as I pass by. "Be the best you can be. Guy at 29 dines here about twice a month, a Du Cœur favorite."

Eyes round and incredulous, but also amused, I say, "No way twice a month."

"Yes, way. Filthy rich, you know. Old money from the California Gold Rush that his family invested profitably."

At this restaurant, the second one I've worked for, the clientele comes from the moneyed class. Privileged with money to spare. Money to put aside for a full-course dinner costing hundreds for two people. And that's without the wine. I could never dine here unless I gave up my apartment, banked all my earnings, and slept in my car or a homeless shelter for a whole week.

Our regular customers are often fifty years or older and established, and come twice, sometimes thrice a year for special occasions. Dining here twice a month? The guy at Table 29 must be worth diamonds to the restaurant.

I get shivers in my spine entering the dining room. I've only been in it when it's empty, quiet, and bright from lights and white tablecloths. This evening, the lighting is subdued and—yes—romantic, warmed by candles and small vases of bright yellow chrysanthemums on tables. Nonintrusive, soft music plays against the hum of voices from every table.

Table 29 usually sits four, but tonight it holds only two people. I'm surprised to see that they're quite young. Maybe about my age or a little older. And attractive. Now I'm even more curious. And intrigued. Mature and rich or nearly rich, I've seen a lot of. But filthy rich and young? Well, I must at least sneak a peek at what this priceless diamond looks like.

For now, though, I'm a willing peon, as grateful as strawberry blond is when I started learning the ropes in this exclusive eatery. So, I focus on the course I'm serving Table 29. How I perform at this restaurant decides whether my career goes haute cuisine or a la Burger King. But that last choice is really no choice at all. I'll work my butt off to make sure it stays that way. It's my future, after all, that I'm slaving for.

I recite to myself the script we've been trained to deliver. The script is quite simple, but this is my first foray into a dining room full of privileged clients. And hives are sprouting on my arms just thinking that I'm serving my creation to the restaurant's most valued client. If this guy doesn't like my dish and blabbers to Laure about it, I can kiss my future in haute cuisine goodbye. Laure is well-loved and well-known, and a word from her can make or break culinary dreams.

I quickly glance, first at his date then at him, vaguely taking in how they look. I take a deep breath, smile at neither one in particular and say, "Medallions of raw ahi, wasabi hollandaise, on a bed of diced cucumbers, vernissage cherry tomatoes, and capers, finished with a sprinkle of toasted nori. Bon appetit!"

Distractedly, my fixed smile still on, I wonder if "filthy rich" Table 29 guy holds my cooking future in his manicured hands—or, more likely, on his pampered taste buds. I take a couple of steps back, so they can start eating. Maybe I can catch a glimpse of whether he likes my dish or not before I go back to the kitchen. I'm also waiting for that "buzz" I've been made to expect. Nothing yet. Anything to say about my creation? Maybe that's what it takes.

But I'm new in this game and still a coward, so I chicken out as he picks up his fork. I control the urge in my legs to run backward to the kitchen. Be at your best, Gina. Be cool. But my ego will be in tatters if Mr. Filthy Rich doesn't like the dish.

A familiar voice, an excited voice, a voice I've not heard from in three years halts my step. "Gina!"

I turn to the woman in surprise. A face I never expected to see in this hallowed hall. I smile, sincerely, but I try to suppress a wide grin at seeing someone I've known since childhood. She's matured nicely—more womanly curves and dark eyes, expertly accentuated. Extra shine in the red-brown hair. Gorgeous in a green dress with a décolletage just low enough to provoke male hands.

My training at this restaurant includes pleasing but sincere decorum with clients—not bright, put-on good cheer. "Cristi, how nice to see you."

Cristi and I grew up in the same neighborhood, but now live in different parts of the city. We see each other only when we happen to visit our respective parents at the same time. My last visit home was two years ago.

She says, "I didn't know this is where you worked. Wow, I'm impressed. Real classy, this place. You must be good."

"I'm just a line cook, but it's great experience. Been here more than a year. How about you? You're looking great. How have you been?"

She beams. "Wonderful, just wonderful. You ... " Her bright smile dims a little.

"Look a little harassed." I chuckle as I finish her sentence. I used to do that a lot for her.

"No, no. You look good. It's just ... "

"How about I call you later, catch up. If you like?"

"Yeah, sure. About time. Same number. You still have it, right?"

"Won't you introduce me to your friend, Cristi?" The male voice turns our heads towards its source. It's deep, relaxed and one you can't ignore.

He's staring at me with a pair of very blue eyes on a well-tanned face crowned by bronze, wavy hair. I bet he's also tall, judging from his long arms. I can easily believe he's filthy rich, as Marcia says. He has that polished, fussed over look you'd never see among the guys in my old neighborhood. Lucky you, Cristi!

I don't feel envy for Cristi—at least envy I will admit to myself. I like guys who are a little more tousled, who clean their fingernails without bothering a manicurist to sculpt them every week. Besides, I'm a realist. This one is way out of my league.

He has a sticky gaze that seems to take in all of me, although his eyes focus on my face. It's been a while since I've had time to go out with men, and I squirm a little at the interest glowing out of Mr. Filthy Rich's eyeballs. In a louder, more insistent voice, he says again, "Introduce us. Cristi?"

Cristi says, "Yeah, sure. Gina, this is Leon."

From the look on Cristi's face, she isn't too happy to introduce me. It had become familiar—her unhappy look. A resentful look I first saw when boys began noticing us.

When she was seventeen, Cristi had her first boyfriend, Paul, whom she met at community college.

Confident that a twenty-year old won't take a girl of fifteen seriously, she introduced him to me. She was wrong. More garrulous and less shy, boys preferred talking to me, and Paul was no exception. Several weeks after I met him, he turned his attention to me. But Cristi said she forgave me.

When her second boyfriend, Bart, dumped her to pursue me, she shed inconsolable tears, wouldn't talk to me for months. I felt bad when she cried and worse when she avoided me. I never hooked up with either Paul or Bart, but that seemed to be beside the point for her. Shifting their attention to me was fault enough. We reconciled on account of our parents being friends, but we couldn't get over that unspoken gulf that sprang up between us.

For the sake of whatever is left of our friendship, I should retreat to the kitchen straightaway, but my niceness training holds me back. Especially because of what this guy means to the restaurant.

Leon rises from his chair and extends a hand to me. I take a couple of steps forward, hesitating a few seconds before I take the proffered hand.

He doesn't shake mine, but covers it with his other hand, squeezes it gently, and gives me a wide smile. "How do you do, Gina? I can't wait to taste your tuna. I'll be sure to tell Laure how I like it."

"Hello, Leon. Nice to meet a friend of Cristi's. I hope you two like the ahi." I withdraw my hand and cast Cristi a surreptitious glance. She's looking down on her plate of sashimi.

More for Cristi's benefit than Leon's, I point to the kitchen, "Gotta go back. Busy, you know. Nice to have met you, Leon. Good to see you again, Cristi. Enjoy the rest of your dinner."

Cristi nods and glances at me with accusing eyes and a forced smile. She picks up her fork and turns her full attention on her plate of sashimi, dismissing me.

Sorry, Cristi. Maybe your guy is a jerk.

Leon sits down, amusement crinkling his eyes. With a small shrug, he also picks up his fork, his sticky, unwavering gaze still on my face. I can feel it following me as I walk back to the kitchen.

Chapter Two

Leon

On a lark, I applied to apprentice at Du Cœur after the manager at the chain restaurant I previously cooked for made a mocking joke—the fry cook had grumbled that orders were coming in too fast. Smirking, the manager said Maybe we'd rather work for Laure Lenoir. He'd heard she was looking around for kitchen peons. He didn't expect any of us to try, much less to be chosen. But he stirred my interest and I thought: What have I got to lose by trying? I'm used to disappointment. Another one—especially one I'm expecting—can't hurt. It can't stop me from dreaming. So, I applied.

Nothing exciting ever happened in the kitchen of that chain restaurant. Its menu probably gets a once-over every twenty years. You could say it's reliable because it's unchanging. It gives customers what they expect year in and year out. For me, though, working there was mind-numbing. I persevered so I could show future employers that I can stick with a job for a while. I was also able to add lines to my resumé, which only filled half a page at the time.

Du Cœur inhabits a totally different world, serving the best of California cuisine. It catapulted to culinary heaven in its first year by capturing the magic of Michelin stars; and for some years now, no other restaurant in the Bay Area east of San Francisco has been able to match its top billing. Its owner, Laure Lenoir, born in France, earned her chops training and slaving in the Charente-Maritime, an area in the coastal region of southwestern France. She came here in her mid-twenties.

Unlike Laure, I'm a nobody from one of those neighborhoods the government chooses to ignore. Rarely does one of us nobodies succeed enough to get to one of those hills where houses have a view of the Golden Gate Bridge. My credentials are limited to a year of culinary arts training at a local community college and one cooking job at the aforementioned chain restaurant.

It's unfair that you can't put home experience in a resumé. I learned everything I truly know about cooking from my mother, whose credentials you can't cite in a resumé, either. But she learned from the best— a French chef who was, in fact, her father. He owned an artisanal French delicatessen where he cooked, vacuum-sealed, and sold ready-to-eat chef's meals you only needed to dunk in boiling water or microwave while still in their packages. It made for gourmet eating in a jiffy. He also made patés and pastries. It was, my grandmother says, a successful venture.

But all the good things of my mother's childhood ended tragically when a gunman went into the delicatessen one night, minutes before closing time, and killed her father.

*****

Not long after I sent Du Cœur my application, I was asked to come in for an interview. The next day, the sous chef called to offer me an apprenticeship, along with two others. They said one of us would be offered the job of a prep cook. Nine months later, I learned that one was me.

Why me? Because, the sous chef said, they want someone they could shape, but who had a natural knack for mixing flavors, a passion for cooking, and an acute sense of smell. He added, with a twisted smile, "and is willing to work their butts off. Laure likes your hungry look."

Later, he told me confidentially that the owner/chef de cuisine wanted to give other women a break in the profession. Laure's attempts to help women may have been what clinched the job for me. The other two apprentices were men, but just as passionate about cooking as I was.

But no matter. I'm in a place I never thought I'd be. I realize I've been luckier than most, and now my future prospects are more than I've dreamed of. All within three years. Who knows if sometime in a not-too-distant future, I can run my own restaurant, like Laure does? Or maybe open a food place of the sort my grandfather operated. But it will be more "fusion" than French cuisine, to reflect my own mixed heritage.

Three days after Leon and Cristi's dinner at the restaurant, I haven't yet called Cristi to catch up. Though I love working at this restaurant, my time is no longer my own, and socializing, except during breaks with Marcia, is next to impossible.

Tonight, I drag my aching limbs out of the restaurant, the last of the line cooks to leave. As usual, although drained of energy, I'm still wound up.

"Hey, wait up." I hear Marcia's voice behind me.

I stop and turn toward her. She's pulling an envelope out of her handbag.

She says, "I almost forgot. Someone gave this to me when I was coming in today. It's for you."

"Me? Who was it?"

Marcia shrugs and hands me an envelope. "Don't know. A secret admirer?"

I return her shrug, refusing her bait to gossip a little.

Before she opens the door to her car, she says, "I guess we'll do this all over again tomorrow. Open that envelope and tell me about it later, okay? Inquiring minds want to know."

I chuckle as I turn the key on my car, an old Nissan my father owned and gave me when I moved out to my own tiny one-room apartment. "There isn't anthrax in it, is there?"

She laughs, shouts back. "Yeah, someone didn't like your ahi. Throw it out, I say."

I don't throw it out. I shove it into my backpack and forget it. At two in the morning, all I can think of is my warm bed. But I'm too hyped-up to fall asleep right away, so I get into the shower over the tub, turn the water on as hot as I can endure, and stand still, waiting for the tension and fatigue to drain out of my muscles and my bones. Out of the shower, I dry my hair a little and crawl into bed for five hours of sleep.

In the morning, I fish for my cellphone to check messages and email. It's all I have time for before I have to get ready to return to the restaurant. I see the unopened envelope buried in my small backpack next to the cellphone.

Those messages and emails are often my only contact with friends and relatives. I religiously start my mornings with them because I know I won't have the time, energy, or even interest to look at them once my workday starts.

But this morning, curiosity about what's in the envelope and who it's from gets the better of my sense of obligation. Relatives and friends can wait. My curiosity demands to be satisfied.

Inside the envelope is a card. It's plain white except for a golden logo at the top, below which is a phone number. The note is short, written in bold strokes with long graceful lines on the tails of letters like "y" and "f". It's beautiful handwriting:

Fancy a cup of coffee? Call me. Please. Laure won't give me your phone number. Love your ahi, btw.

It's signed "Leon."

I can't ignore the fluttering of excitement in my breast while I'm reading the note, and I remember the look Leon gave me three nights ago. Although he was more suave about it than most men I've met, I still felt like he was caressing my body with his eyes. What about Cristi, Leon?

I'm aware that the decent thing to do is ignore the card. Better still, toss it in the trashcan. He's dating a childhood friend I was once very close to, and who I almost lost after her second boyfriend ditched her to pursue me in earnest.

But I can't throw out Leon's card. First, there's the fluttering in my breast. I'm not quite sure what it means. Then there's what the sous chef calls my "curious nature," which he thinks is an asset, but which I sometimes wonder about. Could it work against me one of these days? After working at Du Cœur for nearly two years, the "me" raised in a marginal neighborhood is now curious about what it's like to live with too much money, especially the kind of money Leon is supposed to have.

But what about Cristi, Gina?

What about Cristi? I tell myself she needn't worry. I'm either too busy or too tired for anything but my work at the restaurant. How can you act on a temptation when you have no time for it?

Still, as I drive to the restaurant, the card is all I can think of. At the restaurant, I push it out of my mind as soon as I start work. You can't keep up with the usual anxious frenzy of a high-end restaurant if your mind wanders away from what you're doing.

At break time, Marcia reminds me again about the card as soon as we start our usual, leisurely walk around the block. "You promised to tell me who the card is from."

I don't remember making a promise, but I can't think of any reason why I shouldn't tell her what she seems eager to know. We've been open with each other from the beginning. This time, though, I fudge a little. "Oh, just a customer telling me he likes my tuna dish."

She nods. "That's nice. In the five years I've been in this restaurant, I only got a card like that once. As you know, Laure's the one who gets the personal compliments since customers just post on Yelp. It's nice, though, that she shares it with all of us."

A few paces later, I say, "You remember who your card's from?"

"Guy on Table 29. The first customer you served your tuna to."

"Oh!" I can almost hear myself deflating—the ego that thought Leon found me special. The upstart who hoped her tuna dish was just the beginning of bigger things. But more than those, the dreamer who thought heaven might be within her reach.

"Yeah. He's kinda nice that way. Did yours come from him, too?"

"Yeah," is all I can say.

Back in the kitchen, turning sea scallops on the grill, I begin to feel relief that my card is not special. At least now I can shove it in a drawer without wondering if I've missed something.

I have trouble throwing things away so I've reserved a drawer in my closet for things I'm not quite sure what to do with. When the drawer gets full, I go through the items and throw out those which have lost either their meaning or their usefulness, like the coupons Mom taught me to collect.

Still, I can't help asking Marcia before we part that evening, "Did you answer the card from Table 29?"

"There's a phone number on the card so, yeah, I called to say thank you."

"I guess I should do the same."

"Up to you. Leon is cool. He won't hold it against you if you don't. He knows how stressed we get in our job."

Maybe because of Cristi, I don't call. Or, maybe, I'm afraid of what talking to Leon might induce me to do.

*****

A week later, on a Monday, when the restaurant is closed, someone buzzes my doorbell at ten o'clock. Barely awake, I slither my sluggish body out of bed, snatch the robe draped on the back of the one armchair I own, and drag my bare feet toward the door.

Through my peephole, I glimpse the thin, lined face of a man. A kindly face framed by gray hair. I open the door, but I can't help feeling annoyed. Mondays are when I catch up on sleep; when I don't turn on my alarm clock; when I sometimes choose to pass the day in my nightgown and robe.

He smiles at me, a man of about fifty with perfect white teeth against tanned, craggy skin. I can't help wondering if his teeth are real.

He's clutching a big bouquet of flaming red roses in his hands. "Miss Gina Lambert?"

"Yes?" I say resentfully.

His smile widens as he thrusts the bouquet at me. "For you."

Maybe I look bewildered. Or suspicious. I know I'm scowling. He says, "Don't worry, it's harmless. Comes from someone you can trust." He takes a bow, still grinning, and ambles away. The old guy has a sense of humor, and as foggy as my brain is, it's not lost on me.

I smile as I watch him disappear on the stairs. I'm sorry I was zombified from a night of deep sleep and couldn't thank him for the roses and his good humor. As I close the door, I smell the roses—beautiful but with little fragrance. Too bad. All roses should have that distinct scent no other flowers have. Sad how we now breed it out of them. Looks are mostly what we care about.

Think of where we'd be if we couldn't smell food. We could be eating bad stuff and not know it.

In the kitchen, I put the bouquet in a pitcher of water. The only place where the roses can go is on my all-purpose dining table. I write, eat, drink, and prepare my meals on it.

I reach for the card that came with the roses. But even before I read the card, I get a sneaking suspicion that Leon sent them. One glance at what's written on it tells me I'm right.

What about Cristi, Leon?

And how did you find out where I live?

I'm not listed in the phone book and no one at the restaurant would give Leon my address, I'm pretty sure of that. There's a good reason the staff call Laure "Mother Hen." She's protective. She often says we're like a fraternity or sorority where members must look out for each other. Our unspoken code of honor assumes that we don't rat on our brothers and sisters. So the only way Leon would know where I live is to have me followed. Maybe, by that thin flower messenger. It's really quite easy to do.

It's spooky, though—the thought that I was being followed. Is that, in fact, stalking?

I suppose I should be flattered. Some rich guy, who most women would think themselves lucky to catch, has taken such interest in me that he's going through the trouble of stalking me. Now, he's sending me notes and flowers. But I'm not flattered. I'm angry. Mixed in with that anger is the stirring of fear. It's scary being a victim—I know that from Mom's experience, from classmates who've been robbed, from neighbors whose houses have been broken into.

Maybe I'm being paranoid. Or resentful. More likely, both. The rich think money gives them the freedom to do anything they want, even if it's criminal, and money will protect them from being punished for their crimes. I've never felt that free or that secure. I've always just felt that being poor makes us easy victims.

Chapter Three

Predatory Instinct

Leon is making a play for me. He's rich. I'm poor.

Why me? I can't believe it's my personality or my brains that attract him. True, I think I'm more interesting and brighter than most people give me credit for. But Leon doesn't know me. We've only met once.

Thanks to my looks, maybe? I'm quite pretty, I've been told. More than one old guy has told me I look like Brigitte Bardot who I know only from pictures I once googled. I do have a French grandfather—that, I think, is all I have in common with the seductive Miss Bardot.

My mirror does tell me I have dark lush hair, creamy skin, large blue eyes, a generous mouth, and— Mom says—a straight noble nose like Gwyneth Paltrow's. And a 5'7" body with curves in the right places. You wouldn't call me voluptuous, though. Even so, I may invade many men's fantasies. So my guess is, for Leon, it's lust at first sight—that physical thing people mistake for love. Lust and a rich man's predatory instinct.

I think beauty doesn't get you very far. If you're poor, an average student, with modest ambition (or none at all)—ordinary in every other way—beauty is actually a liability. I find it downright annoying to have men constantly trying to grope me. There have been many, from men with dirty hands to men with manicured fingernails. They all only want one thing. Quite humiliating.

So, I have resolved not to dwell on my looks. I've kept my focus on the one thing my mother knows best, that she's passed on to me—cooking.

My mom's mom was too young when she married. She had a bit of money after my grandfather died, but when that was all used up, she and her three kids subsisted on welfare. My mother, the oldest, worked at fast food restaurants as soon as she was old enough and before she could finish high school.

Her father's talent (or his passion for food) must have rubbed off on Mom, though. She had spent days at her father's delicatessen from the age of four because Grandma was the cashier and her kids went with her. Mom began helping her father as early as she could remember, fetching utensils and ingredients. By nine years old, she was helping him cook.

Maybe, it's natural that she's turned into a great cook. She delights in cobbling together the best possible dinner out of the everyday ingredients our family can afford. Because her mother is Chinese, her dishes are sometimes French, sometimes Chinese and many times a mix of both. And they're always scrumptious.

Mom's dinners have kept our family together. How can you take offense or be angry at people with whom you've just shared a great meal? Even as teenagers, when we preferred to hang out with friends, we ran home every evening for Mom's dinners. We couldn't always tell what she'd serve. But we knew it would be delicious.

For Mom, cooking is life. She keeps her family happily well fed, for sure. But maybe more than that, cooking helps her escape the grubby, grinding realities of each day, at least for the few hours she prepares her dishes and watches us eat.

Do I have the passion Mom has—one that doesn't ask for or expect rewards? Not money, not even words of thanks or appreciation. Like Mom, I believe I inherited Grandpa's desire to create something that can make people feel good. That can give not only life, but meaning to it. Starting with Grandpa, that something is food. Dishes we try to bump up from the ordinary. But can I sustain that passion like Mom does?

As much as I love Mom, though, and as much in awe as I am of her cooking talent, I don't want to end up like her. It took me a while to realize this. Lucky for me, I came to this point just in time—a point in which I chose to take care of myself, instead of having someone take care of me.

Growing up, I bought the idea of living for love and a family. It was for them that I'd cook. And for some years, I went looking for happiness with some man. Since people thought I was high on the much valued beauty scale, I assumed I ought to be destined for something extraordinary. Like bagging some rich Adonis who would shower me with all I could ask for.

But Fate didn't quite see it that way. For one, I haven't seen any Adonis out there. Anyway, all he is is a character in Greek mythology hatched by someone's great imagination.

My parents are not what privileged outsiders would call "nice." They're not nasty, but they could seem indifferent. I admit that, except for those dinners, I believe they've been neglectful. Not because they care little for their children. It's more that they neither have time nor energy to show how much they care. They're too harassed by all the things it takes to live—menial jobs, more children than they can afford and handle, etc. They wear their stresses, their apparent lack of caring on their scowls, and when Mom is too tired, she also wears it on her tightly drawn lips.

I have wondered how much my mother has been affected by her father's murder and the poverty her family endured afterward. Grandma was only eighteen when she married, and when she was widowed, she had few employable skills—none, I believe, that would have earned her enough to support her children.

As I grew up, my parents couldn't be bothered to inspire us to dream. They once told us all they asked is for their children not to get into drugs and crime; and if possible, for my sister Sabine and me to marry men who could support us in comfort. They had neither the money nor the desire to dream high for themselves, and they never expected their children to aim high, either. So, while I did quite well in English and math without working too hard, I did average work in every other class and thought myself quite ordinary, brain-wise. College—where I might have taken a more ambitious path—never occurred to me as an option. So before I turned to cooking to keep myself in reasonable comfort, I went full throttle into a quest for love, family, and a good home. One better than my parents gave me.

Right after high school, I lived for dates, going out with a string of men to find my destiny. Finally, at nineteen, I met a truly nice man at the house of Cristi's boss. Cristi—shy and slow to make friends—asked me to go with her for "moral support". I was thrilled, thinking that at that wealthy house, I might meet "better" people and—who knows?—the extraordinary destiny due me.

Cristi is a dental assistant to a successful dentist. He's probably not what most people would call rich but he and his family live in a gated community with homes four times the size of my family home. That I thought them wealthy, at that age, goes to show how little I knew about what it's like to have much more money than you actually need to survive.

Anyway, I did meet someone that night at the dentist's house. Someone who changed my life, but not in the way I had anticipated.

Adam wasn't Adonis, but he wasn't bad looking and he was good in bed. With a college degree, a steady job, and raised in a close-knit middle-class family, I was sure he'd make a good husband and father. And he did something other guys I dated rarely did—he brought me flowers. A bouquet, now and then, and a single rose every time we saw each other. After several months of going out with him, he asked me to marry him.

I was actually dumbfounded when he "popped the question," and for a few minutes, I stayed silent, a blank look on my face. Here was the destiny I had been waiting for—being offered to me with a bouquet of two dozen roses when I was barely twenty. And yet, from the moment he uttered the first word of his proposal, I knew I was going to say "No."

I did love him, although one might say not enough. The prospect of rejecting him pained me. I would be hurting him, yes; but I was probably hurting myself more. Someone like him might never come my way again, in the forgotten world I lived in.

When, finally, "No" croaked out of my throat, I could tell he was more shocked than I was. He was one hundred per cent sure I'd say yes. He stared at me for a long time, saying nothing. Then, he got up and walked away, his hands bunched up in his pockets.

He didn't try to persuade me of his love or change my mind about my answer. Maybe, he sensed that I'd stick to my "No" no matter what he did. Or, maybe, he thought there were many more girls like me out there, so why waste another minute on me. I haven't seen him since.

Why—when I had the chance to have the future I envisioned for myself—did I not seize it? I had endured groping from many men to find that one person who could give me the life I thought I was owed. I really believed from the first time Adam asked me out that he would be that one.

That very night, after a mere hour or so later, regretting what might have been, I stayed up planning what I should do for the next few years, if not for the rest of my life. I told myself that God or Fate was giving me a signal when I said "No" to Adam. A chance to make something more of myself than just a better version of my mother.

That "No" was like an epiphany, but not with angels tooting their horns. Mine rose out of pain, out of a constant state of wanting what I imagined I could never have, what I thought a lot of other people took for granted.

At twenty, I had no burning ambition, not even a vague idea of where I wanted to be ten years from now. But it became crystal clear that I needed to change the path I had been expected to take. I needed to take control of my future. At the very least, I needed to make a living that not only paid more than cleaning hotel rooms, which was what my mother has done since I was little. I need some sense that I matter. That I am more than just a face and a body, good for making babies, keeping my family fat and happy, and cleaning noses and asses along with toilets, furniture, and floors.

I asked myself what I could do well and actually liked. The following week I enrolled in cooking classes at the community college. It wasn't an earth-shaking step, but it would take me nearer to a certain kind of freedom. And towards something I hadn't dreamed about until now.

Chapter Four

Jealousy

The bouquet of red roses is not the last one Leon sends me. Every week after that, the same thin, smiling old guy comes bearing another bouquet of the same kind of roses on the same day and at the same time. A card comes with each bouquet, but most of the time, except for his signature and his phone number, Leon doesn't scribble a greeting or a note on it. After the note accompanying the first roses, he wrote twice: "I'll keep sending flowers until you agree to see me."

I know when that particular note comes on the third week of roses that I should call to ask him to stop sending me the roses, but I don't know exactly what and how to say it so that I sound convincing. Besides, I really don't know what to say to a spoiled, filthy rich guy, educated at the best schools. Marcia tells me he has an MBA from some place called Haas Business School in Berkeley. And, yet, how hard can it be if Cristi can talk to him? I should ask her. It will only take a phone call. But will she be suspicious and resentful if she and Leon are still dating? Especially after the history she and I have with her former boyfriends.

That leaves Marcia.

Marcia doesn't speak for a minute or two after I tell her about the roses. Then, she says, "You say he's dating a friend of yours?"

"Yeah, Cristi. She was his date the night I served the ahi. Cristi and I grew up together. Our family homes are on the same block. We were best friends once, but we only see each other now when we happen to visit our parents at the same time."

"So, you're asking Leon to stop sending those flowers because of her. Would you go out with him if she wasn't in the picture?"

Her question makes me pause. I'm no longer angry at Leon but I still resent the stalking. So I surprise myself when I say, "Well, it's tempting. I've never gone out with a rich guy."

I meant it to be a funny answer. I didn't expect Marcia to take it seriously. But she does.

"Does it bother you if I tell you Leon is a skirt-chaser, a court-em, leave-em kind of guy? He loves the pursuit, and my guess is he's never been in love. He's probably getting tired of your friend already and looking for a new diversion."

"Marcia, I was kidding." Was I? "But how do you know all this?"

"I've worked in this restaurant long enough, and I hear things."

I look at Marcia thoughtfully. "Did you ever go out with him?"

"I'm not his type. He's four years younger than me."

"But you're young and attractive."

"Yeah, 33, and ten pounds overweight. I'm still looking for that special person who'll overlook my flaws because he loves my pastries. Anyway, here's my advice: Keep the flowers coming and wait until he leaves your friend."

"That sounds crass and devious."

"Why? You want to know what it's like going out with a filthy rich guy. Well, here's your chance. Just remind yourself always what his intentions are and don't get emotionally involved. Have fun and enjoy the ride for as long as it lasts."

"It's Cristi I'm actually thinking of."

"Cristi is a big girl, although I hope for her sake she's not expecting more out of Leon than he's willing to, or can give."

On the drive home from work that night, I mull over Marcia's question: Would you go out with him if she wasn't in the picture?

My answer was silly but it makes me wonder. Leon does intrigue me, or maybe, his money and its accompanying privileges do. It doesn't hurt that he is, in fact, quite attractive.

I do nothing to stop the flowers from coming.

*****

Two months later, I go home for Thanksgiving, which I've not been able to do the past two years because of my restaurant duties. This year, though, I take the week off, since I've been assigned to the Christmas Eve dinner. I'm sure that, like me, Cristi is also spending this holiday with her family. We've both done so since we left home.

I call her on Wednesday. "Cristi, it's me. Gina."

"Oh, hi! You at home?"

"Yes. I got a holiday break. No cooking for a week. Yeaay!"

"Haven't seen you around here for quite a while."

"Haven't got time for myself. That restaurant keeps me too busy for anything else. I'm sorry I couldn't call you until now. Can I come see you, or you can come see me, catch up?"

I get silence for what seems like a couple of minutes. It's probably not that long but I do wonder and feel uneasy about it.

Finally, Cristi says, "I think that'd be great. How about Thursday afternoon? Everybody will be watching football and no one will disturb us in my room."

Cristi sounds eager to talk and I suspect it's because she wants to brag about Leon.

On Thursday after the usual "great to see you" greetings that come with pretend busses on the cheeks, she takes my hand and leads me to the bedroom she shares with her younger sister.

She closes the door, saying, "So no one comes barging in on us. It's the signal me and Joana use to say we want privacy. We can make ourselves comfortable on my bed."

I follow her toward her bed where we both sit, cross-legged; me, leaning on the headboard, and she on the opposite end.

"Tell me how you got to cook at that restaurant. I thought by now you'd be married and pregnant with Adam's kid. So I was shocked last time I talked to your mom. She said you were a cook at Country Kitchen. She didn't seem too unhappy, though. I know it was her ambition to get you nicely settled and I'm sure she thought Adam was a great catch. We all did."

"He did ask me. I'm still not sure why I turned him down. Maybe, I wanted to find my own place in the big, bad world. Me, on my own. Or maybe cooking is just in our blood, you know, through the French grandfather I never met."

"Maybe that's it. Really tragic, what that criminal did to him. But it looks like you're following his footsteps now. Lucky you, cooking at Du Cœur."

"Yeah, that's another thing I'm still not quite sure about—why Laure picked me. I apprenticed there, at first. Came in with two guys who I believed were better than me. When I asked the sous chef, he just said, 'consider yourself fortunate. Many pass by through these hallowed walls. Only a very small handful stay.'"

"I've always thought you were lucky."

"There's luck, for sure. But I couldn't leave it at that. I really needed to know, maybe because I didn't have any confidence in what I could do. So, a few days later, I bugged him some more. So then he says they could tell I've got this passion for creating dishes and that I work my butt off. But so do those two guys who were hired with me. So I think it's because I'm a woman. Laure is known to champion female chefs. She's doing all she can to get more of us cooking in restaurants like hers."

"Like I said, you're lucky. Lucky in love, lucky in work." Cristi scowls at me, her smile fading. "I've always envied you. You seem to get things you want all the time and without much effort."

"But I'm working my ass off now. The restaurant owns me, body and mind. I never get time for myself anymore. Lady Luck is with you now, Cristi. Marcia, the pastry chef at the restaurant tells me Leon is filthy rich. He looks really good, too."

Cristi turns her face away from me. "You should have married Adam. That would have solved all our problems."

I'm puzzled. I thought she'd welcome the chance to talk and brag about Leon. What can she mean by her remark? I ignore it. "Believe me, if you saw me working at the restaurant, you'd think me stupid, or bonkers, or I'm on hard labor like I'm being punished."

"You chose where you are now. How could you reject Adam?" Cristi's eyes are beginning to squint the way I've seen them when she's on the verge of anger; like those times in the past when she accused me of attracting her boyfriends away from her. "You should have married him. And you shouldn't have brought Leon up."

Cristi doesn't want to talk about Leon. Marcia must be right that he has grown tired of her. Is it for my own self-interest that I mentioned Leon?

Leon is getting to me. Or, at least, those flowers he sends that brighten my cheerless apartment. I know I must ask him to stop sending them because he's still dating Cristi. Maybe I need a push. I thought seeing Cristi brag about Leon was that push.

Still, I have to ask myself: Am I hoping Marcia is right that Leon might be tired of Cristi by now?

I frown and bite my lip, feeling uneasy at my thoughts. I drag my butt towards Cristi and grasp her arm to force her to look at me. I can see hatred in her eyes and pangs of guilt hit me. For hoping Marcia is right. For having brought up Leon—it now seems so scheming of me. For whatever part I played in ruining Cristi's love life. Can I atone for any of them?

"Cristi, is there something you want to tell me?" Maybe I'm hoping she'll let her anger out by shouting and accusing me like she had done before.

But in a low soft voice, she says "I think you know."

"No. How could I? I've had no time for anything else but work. Not much time for talking except at break. I've got no new friends, much less a boyfriend." Am I actually trying to tell her she's now the lucky one?

"No, you don't need to go after them, friends or boyfriends. They always just come after you, like duck to water." Cristi is squinting even harder. If she started out trying to be nice to me today, her anger has now taken over.

I let go of her arm and swing my legs off the bed. "I think I should go now."

"Not before you hear me out."

I swing my legs back up and move my butt back towards the headboard. I wish I could just run out of the room. "I'm here, Cristi, and all ears. I didn't mean to upset you."

"No? This isn't the first time you've done this to me. By my own count, this is the third."

"I don't understand."

"Yes, you do. First, Paul. Then, Bart. Now it's Leon."

"But I didn't do anything to take them away from you."

"No, you didn't. They only have to take one look at you and I've lost them."

"I never encouraged them. Bart tried to win you back."

"I couldn't forgive him for leaving me for you. By then, I thought of him as a discard. I wouldn't take a discard back."

"I'm truly sorry, Cristi."

"I'm sorry, too. But I'll never forgive you for Leon. Things were going great between us until he saw you at the restaurant. We kept dating and I thought he maybe forgot about you. But looks like I was wrong."

"I don't know what he's told you, but I never answered any of the notes he's been sending me."

45

"Notes? He's sent you notes? He said he's been sending you flowers."

"He told you that?"

"Yes, 'in the spirit of full disclosure,' he says. But he lied about the notes."

"The notes came with the flowers."

"I should have guessed. He went after me the way he's going after you. I didn't know he'd been sending you flowers until just a week ago when he broke up with me. Said he couldn't stop thinking about you and couldn't keep seeing me anymore. Then, he told me about the flowers. But he never said anything about notes. I thought I was the only one he wrote notes to with the flowers he sent. He didn't tell me everything."

"Maybe he just didn't want to tell you I've pretty much ignored them."

"You said that about Paul and Bart, too. That you ignored whatever it was they did to get you to go out with them. Didn't do much good."

I say nothing but I can't look at Cristi. I can feel her intense, angry gaze on me.

She gets up as she says, "What's it about you, Gina? I'm pretty, too. So many people have said they prefer my looks to yours."

I glance quickly at her. "You're beautiful, and those people are right."

"But I'm not beautiful like you."

"Maybe men are just jerks, Cristi."

"No, it isn't that. Doesn't help to think that. Hurts no matter what. Being dumped hurts an awful lot. And for someone who's supposed to be your friend. ..." She turns and walks away from the bed.

I want to run out of the room but I can't. Not while Cristi is in the state she's in. Not with the guilt I feel. In my more clear-thinking moments, I feel it's unfair of her to blame me for her inconstant boyfriends and yet I also can't help feeling responsible for her unhappiness. I don't move from my perch on the bed.

She turns around to face me again. "All the pain I've suffered—all because of you."

"I'm sorry, Cristi. I never meant to hurt you."

I never saw it coming—what happens next. I see her rushing toward me. She raises her arm and before I can grasp what she's up to, I feel a sharp point digging into my right shoulder. I scream, more out of shock, than out of pain.

But the pain comes, piercing, slicing through my shoulders, intensifying. Cristi raises her arm again. She has a pair of scissors in her hand. There's blood on it and on her hand. My blood!

I scream louder, scrambling quickly away from her, and shielding my body with my arms. By the time I jump to the other side of the bed, the door flies open and her whole family runs into the room.

Several voices shout at the same time. "Oh, no, Cristi, what have you done?"

One of her brothers grabs her arm from behind and pries the scissors out of her hand.

Cristi's parents run toward me and her mother shouts, "Ronny, call 911."

I can feel warm liquid dripping down my bare arm. I stare at my shoulder and arm. So red; so much blood.

My legs are melting from underneath me, but an arm catches me and lays me gently on the bed. Someone's face hovers over my own. I think it's Cristi's dad. He presses a piece of cloth on my shoulder and I gasp. He says, "Sorry to hurt you but I'm trying to stop the bleeding. Hang in there. An ambulance should be here in a couple of minutes."

The pain in my shoulders is slowly easing into a throbbing numbness. I close my eyes, and voices around me fade away. Silence can be so comforting.

Chapter Five

Hurt

I open my eyes inside an ambulance. My shoulder feels numb but at least it's not hurting anymore. I say to the paramedic sitting to my right, "Am I still bleeding?"

"No. You passed out from fear, shock. Just a few minutes. You lost some blood, but not as much as it looked. Don't worry, they'll patch you up good. We're almost there."

At the hospital, they put me on a gurney and wheel me directly to a room blazing with lights. People in shapeless blue garb, caps, and surgical masks fuss over me, sticking needles into my arm and wrapping monitors around it.

I close my eyes. I can't believe this is happening to me. I'm supposed to be relaxing, waiting until my mother calls me to dinner. She says I need time away from pots and pans and refused my help in the kitchen. *Can't I rewind my life like a film, back to before I call Cristi?*

An efficient voice breaks into my thoughts. "Can you breathe well enough?"

"Yes," I say, glancing up at the woman with the efficient voice. I see only her eyes.

She puts an oxygen mask on half my face; and as cool liquid courses down my arm, she fades into blackness.

A smiling, maternal face is saying something—about me, I think. "Everything went well. We just finished stitching and bandaging your wound. We had to probe about a bit. The scissors were blunt. They left an ugly wound and grazed your shoulder blade, but luckily the wound didn't go deeper. No serious harm done, although we'll have to wait to see if there's some nerve damage. If so, it may take a few weeks to have full use of your right arm again."

I force myself to say "thank you," but all I remember is "no serious harm." That's all I need, to know that I can go back to life, as usual.

"We're keeping you overnight, at least. I think we'll be able to discharge you tomorrow. We're just waiting for hospital aides to take you to your room."

A day in the hospital. What about Thanksgiving? "Are my parents here?"

"Yes. They've been informed about your room number so you'll see them there."

Sometime later, my parents come into the room. Mom is scowling, her eyes dark with worry. "Thank God, you're okay. How are you feeling?" She pulls a chair next to the bed.

"Groggy. My shoulder is sore."

Dad stands at the foot of the bed. "The restaurant is paying medical insurance. What a relief. Never thought I needed to set aside money for this."

Mom leans over to stroke my forehead and my hair. I don't remember her ever doing that before. "The doctor says everything will be fine."

Dad says, "Yeah, we're glad you're okay. Not much harm done, I hope."

I say, "The doctor says nothing serious."

"The hospital must have reported the stabbing. Got a call from Maurice half an hour ago. He saw the police at the Silvas. Took Cristi with them, maybe for questioning. What's going on between you two?"

"I think she just lost it. She came at me. Then, I saw blood staining my blouse and she was raising her arm. She had a pair of scissors. I put my arms up over my head, scooted over quickly to the other side of the bed, away from her. That was when people came running in. I was screaming at the top of my lungs."

Dad shakes his head. "Never can see why anyone should get so worked up over anything. Attacking a friend. That's crazy."

Mom says, "I thought you were just doing catch-up because you two haven't seen each other in a while. Next thing we know, Joanna comes barging into the house, shouting you've been hurt. I ask her how but she couldn't tell us. Just kept shouting you were hurt. We rush after her, see you lying on the bed. Blood on you. I tell you, all that fear, that anguish when I was a child ... when the police came." Mom bites her lips; her mouth quivers as it always does when she recalls her father's murder.

"Oh Mom, I'm sorry."

"What's there to be sorry about? I was scared, but then I got angry. Not at you but at that whole family. It actually felt good, blowing up like that. All this anger in me—just exploded."

"Your mom was like a volcano, shouting, 'What have you done to my daughter? What have you done to my daughter?' She pushed Raf away and he fell on his butt. I've never seen your Mom so angry. Or Raf looking so ridiculous on the floor." Dad starts laughing.

Mom says, "Raf tried to apologize, told us an ambulance was on its way. But I was still too angry so I shoved him away from you."

"You should have seen the Silvas cowering in their boots. Trixie tried to hand Julie a clean piece of cloth but Julie snarled at her, told her to stay away. So everyone stood frozen in place. Then, the ambulance arrived."

Mom resumes stroking my hair. "I looked at you, watched your chest going up and down; somehow I knew you'd be okay. So, I began to calm down."

Dad says, "What was Cristi so angry about?"

"Something she thinks I've done."

Mom says, "What is it? What did you do to her?"

"I didn't do anything. We were talking, that's all. She's very unhappy about something and she's blaming me for it."

"But why would she blame you?"

"Mom, I can't tell you much more about what's going on in Cristi's head."

Dad says, "Let her be. She needs to rest. It looks like the police are investigating. Maybe we'll find out later what's going on in that girl's head."

Mom says, "I can't understand it. Cristi has always been such a nice, well-behaved child, with that pretty smile on her face, like nothing ever goes wrong for her."

Shortly before noon the next day, my whole family arrives. My youngest brother Bernie, who is 12, runs to me, hugs me and won't let go for a few minutes. Sabine, four years younger than me, tugs at his arm. "My turn."

Bernie lets go. After Sabine, Gerard—a year younger than Sabine, and Maurice, a year older—take their turn. I'm overwhelmed but deeply touched. There's never been so much hugging in my family. We're pretty laid back. When another family member joins us in a room, we may nod, but often, we simply take no notice of it.

The hospital releases me a couple of hours later. In the car, Mom yields the choice front passenger seat to me. She squeezes in the back seat with my sister and three brothers. Bernie sits on my mother's lap. Everyone is being solicitous and it feels good.

Later, at home, Cristi's parents come to see me. My parents and the Silvas seem to have made up.

Mr. Silva says, "Truly sorry, Gina. We're shocked—what Cristi did to you. We can't explain it. The police came, took her away yesterday. She didn't come home. She's suicidal, they say. They put her in a hospital for observation."

Mr. Silva is scowling, but his wife, sitting next to him, is turning redder beneath her ruddy skin. Shame over what Cristi did to me? Or Cristi's being put in a psychiatric hospital?

Somehow, I'm not surprised Cristi is suicidal, but it's sad, bewildering. I can't imagine what it's like being so unhappy that you'd want to kill yourself.

Trixie Silva bursts out crying and my Mom and I watch her. Mr. Silva and my father look away. We all wait, saying nothing, doing nothing, until Mrs. Silva stops crying. "I'm okay," she says, drying her eyes with tissue Mom hands her.

A couple of minutes later, the Silvas leave.

After they've gone, Dad says, "Cristi's gone bonkers. That family's in for some tough months ahead. If the police charge Cristi with assault, they'll have to fork out a pretty penny to hire a lawyer."

He doesn't expect either me or Mom to say what we think of his take on recent events. In his mind, what happened is now clear to him and he's content.

He pats my hand and says, "Well, rest up. You'll be as good as new in a couple of weeks or so." Then, he leaves the room. We hear him turning on the television.

Mom stays and sits on the edge of my bed. "What's Cristi so unhappy about, Gina?"

I shrug my shoulders and don't say anything.

Mom isn't satisfied with my silence. She watches me and waits. She'll sit there until I give her some explanation.

I relent and tell her about Leon and Cristi coming to the restaurant for dinner. I also mention the flowers, and the break-up, but not Leon's excuse for it.

She says when I finish, "Trixie told me about that young man. She was swelling with pride, seemed sure it was serious. Maybe Cristi gave a false impression. He can't be that nice if he was sending you flowers while he was dating her. Did you make it clear to him you weren't interested?"

"I said nothing, did nothing, just ignored all of it."

"Why? That's not good, Gina. You interested in this Leon?"

"Well, how often does a very rich, good-looking guy send you flowers every week? The whole year I was with Adam, he brought me a bunch of flowers once in a while. That was very nice, but it still can't compare with every week. Yeah, so I admit I was intrigued."

Mom shakes her head. "Your Dad never gave me flowers. They're dressing, that's all. How much do you know Leon?"

"Not much. Only what people at the restaurant say about him. Marcia, our pastry chef, says he's a playboy and will tire of Cristi sooner or later. When he does, and if he still wants to go out with me, Marcia says I should say yes. Have fun, so long as I expect nothing more."

"That's not good, either."

"But why, Mom? If I do, I'll treat him the way he's treating me. Why can't I have fun? I work my butt off enough."

"It's not what I've taught you."

"But that's so old-fashioned, expecting a man to take care of me. Look what happened to Grandma. And it didn't stop with her."

I thought Mom would be angry at what I said, but it's time she accepts that I mean to do something else with my life than just marry and have babies. I'm not sure yet what I want to do about Leon if he persists, but Marcia has a point. Why can't women enjoy men and sex without commitment?

Mom stares at me, doesn't speak for some minutes.

"Okay. You're an adult and can take care of yourself. I can also see you want to try things out. And I know you'll do what you want to do. Doesn't matter what I say. But be careful. I'd be sorry to see you hurt, to turn out like Cristi."

"Thank you, Mom, for understanding. I'll be careful not to end up like her."

"Cristi may have gone bonkers; like your Dad says. But I can't approve of her attacking you. Violence never fixes anything."

"I guess no one can tell what a person would do in anger, not even someone you think is your friend."

Shaking her head once more, Mom gets up. "Go to sleep. You need rest. I saved you some Thanksgiving dinner so when you're starved, just holler. I'll bring it to you. You need food to heal."

Chapter Six

Healing

I wake up before noon the next day. Sabine says I've been asleep twenty hours. No wonder I'm starved. My last bite of food was at lunch, before I visited Cristi. Intravenous feeding at the hospital doesn't count. Food is something you chew taste, savor, and swallow.

Remembering the Thanksgiving dinner Mom saved for me, I shout, though I doubt my parched throat carries my words too far out of the room, "I'm hungry."

Sabine saunters in, book in hand. "I'll heat the plate Mom set aside for you."

She comes back minutes later, carrying a tray with a steaming plate of food. She sets it on a small desk that doubles as my night table. "Can you sit up?"

I nod. "Yes, but help me. My shoulder's heavy as lead. Hurts a bit."

"Wait. Can you hold yourself up a little?"

I nod again.

She takes the pillow from her bed, piles it on top of mine, and helps me lean back against them. She takes the tray and pulls out its legs, positioning it like a bridge over my thighs.

I smile at Sabine. Whatever else my family is, we do what we can when one of us needs help. Maybe because of my mother, we take care not to hurt each other. When we were kids, Cristi once told me her father used his belt on her brothers whenever they did something bad. She tried to be good and she'd never been hit. My father has never laid a hand on any of us.

Mom walks in while I'm eating. Sabine has cut the turkey breast into pieces.

Mom says, "How are you feeling this afternoon? You sure slept."

"I'm good. Sore in my chest, and up and down my left arm."

"It's not numb is it, your arm? Because if it is, the doctor says you'll have to stay off work for a while longer."

I pinch a few spots on my left arm. "No, I don't think so. There's feeling along my arm. I almost forgot about work."

Sabine says, "Don't worry. Mom asked me to call. I couldn't get through to the restaurant but you gave Mom Marcia's number so I called her. Good thing you did that."

"So you told Marcia?"

"Yes, she said not to worry. She'll tell the restaurant and she'll call you tomorrow. Seems like a nice lady; sounded like she really cared about you."

"If I have a best friend in that place, it's Marcia. She's older, much more experienced, frank. Gives me advice like an older sister."

Before long, my father stomps into the room, rubbing his stomach round and round with his palm. He grins at me, "Good. You're up and eating like a pig. And here I am with a growling stomach. I've got two great cooks in this house and there's no food to be had."

Mom gets up and says, "Come along. I'll make you a hamburger with lots of sautéed onions." She looks back at me. "I'll be back to talk to you later."

When they've left, I turn to Sabine. "Has anyone heard anything more about Cristi?"

"She's coming home Monday. But I heard they may charge her with ... battery, I think, is what her mom said."

But she wasn't thinking right, just hurting a lot."

"I don't think it's for you to say what authorities decide to do."

An hour later, Mom returns. "How did you like your mashed potatoes?"

"Loved them. But you did something different. You couldn't have mixed celery in but they smell a bit like celery."

"It's celery root, boiled and mashed with potatoes. I'd almost forgotten about it, but cooking for that restaurant, you've inspired me; brought back some memories. Celery root is not cheap, but I thought: Thanksgiving. Why not splurge?"

"I think they're wonderful together. Maybe, you'll have more great memories of food you can share with me."

"We'll see. But that's for another day."

"Heard anything more about Cristi?"

"She's still at that hospital—some kind of psychiatric care facility."

"How is she?"

"A lot calmer, Trixie says. They put her on some kind of drug. It seems Cristi has been staying alone in her room a lot since she came home for this visit. But Trixie says she's always been so quiet anyway. Not like Joanna. So no one thought anything was wrong."

"I wonder when they'll let her out."

Mom shrugs. "Who knows? Trixie says she may be charged with battery."

Chapter Seven

The Lieutenant

On Monday morning, a detective knocks on our door. He arrives mid-morning and he's waiting for me in the living room. He rises as I walk in, a tall man of about thirty who fills his blue jeans, white shirt opened at the neck, and dark casual suit jacket with palpable strength. He has that familiar spark I've seen in many men's eyes when they see me for the first time. But it dies as quickly as it lights up. He doesn't goggle at me like others have done. Like Leon did. But he doesn't look away in embarrassment, either.

He extends a hand and I take it. He has a warm and comforting grip. "Miss Regine Lambert? I'm Lieutenant Hansen of the Oakland Police Department."

"Gina please. It was my mother's choice to call me Regine but I never use it. I don't actually like the name."

He doesn't smile, but amusement creeps into his eyes. As we sit down across from each other, he says "I'm sorry to bother you while you're recovering from your injuries but I need to ask you some questions about the stabbing incident."

"No, no bother. But I want to tell you up front I don't want Cristi charged."

"Unfortunately, that's not up to you. Nor me. I'm just gathering evidence and the district attorney decides."

"What do you want me to tell you?"

"Let's start with your version of what happened. You don't mind if I record it in my phone, do you?"

"No, I don't mind."

I give him my story, in as much detail as I can remember. He doesn't interrupt and his gaze is so direct I have to avert mine sometimes. But I can't tell how much of my story he believes. Maybe cultivating a deadpan face goes with his job.

"Thank you," he says when I finish. His gaze travels down to something on the floor which he scowls at. My parents have never bothered to replace the living room rug; it's shabby, worn thin from years of use. I think they're just waiting for the wood underneath to show before they strip it off completely. The detective's absorption in it makes me uncomfortable.

He glances up again and, for the first time, I'm struck by how sad his eyes look. They're gray and piercing, under unexpectedly long and thick lashes that make that sad look sadder still. Why did I not see that right away? It couldn't have been the rug that brought it on. What demons could be lurking in this man's breast?

"You called Miss Cristi Silva's former boyfriend Leon. Is that Leon of the rich Barrett family?"

"Yes. Do you know him?"

"A little. Do you like Miss Silva, Miss Lambert? Does she like you?"

His questions catch me off-guard for a few moments. "Yes, of course. I like her. I believe she likes me, too."

"But she stabbed you with a pair of scissors."

"She was distraught."

"About the breakup with Leon Barrett?"

"That's what I said."

"Which she blamed you for. Do you think it's unfair of her to do so?"

"Wouldn't you think so, if you didn't do anything?"

"You didn't ask Mr. Barrett to stop sending you the flowers."

"They brightened my apartment. I can see now that's a mistake. But would it have prevented Cristi from stabbing me if I stopped the flowers?"

He doesn't answer my question, but he smiles—the first he's given me. He puts his cell phone in his shirt pocket. "Thank you again for patiently answering my questions. I've no more for the moment. But it's likely some new ones will come up so I'll probably have to talk to you again."

"Sure. I'm going nowhere and I believe my dad has given you my phone number. May I ask what'll happen to Cristi?"

"I honestly can't say, Miss Lambert. The stabbing qualifies as either assault or battery but there's always extenuating circumstances."

Something about the lieutenant's eyes stays with me and I can't help wanting to know what it could be.

*****

Cristi visits me the following day, chaperoned by her mother. At first, I wonder why Mrs. Silva came, but I understand why when we settle ourselves in the living room—me with my mother and she with hers. My mother joined us when she saw Mrs. Silva enter behind Cristi.

Cristi's eyes look glazed and her mind seems to be far away. She's moving like a zombie and I think it's the drug they've given her. She can hardly open her mouth to greet me. Once seated, she stutters her apologies for hurting me. But her words sound rehearsed. All I can do is sit and wish all over again that we could go back to the day before Thanksgiving.

After some uncomfortable minutes where nobody can think of anything to say, I try small talk and ask a question foremost in my mind—one I'll also have to answer for myself. And soon. "When does your leave end, Cristi? When are you going back to work?"

She looks at her mother, who answers for her. "We've called her work. She'll stay home for another week."

I say, "I may have to do the same. My work needs strength and stamina, and my shoulders are still swollen."

Cristi knits her brow and turns her face away.

I say, "I think it's a good thing to stay home for a while. I need rest. I've been driving myself hard for the last three years."

Mom says, grinning, "We're quite happy to have you here, imposing on us a little longer. Haven't seen much of you these last two years. When you're a little better, maybe you can cook some fancy restaurant dish."

Mom gives Mrs. Silva a wink which Mrs. Silva answers with an uneasy smile. I know Mom is doing her best to reassure mother and daughter that what happened is just another one of those incidents that can happen among neighbors. It'll pass and we'll all go on as before.

Mom means well, but her effort to rebuild a bridge that's still burning upsets Cristi. She bolts from her chair and runs toward the door, crying, her hands on her face.

Mrs. Silva bounces from her seat and runs after Cristi. She bangs the front door closed behind her.

Surprised but not necessarily puzzled, Mom and I look at each other. After a couple of silent minutes, she says, "I think the coffee is ready. I guess I only have to bring two cups."

Mom calls me weeks later to tell me that Mrs. Silva has been trying to avoid her. And I don't see Cristi again for a long time.

Chapter Nine

Time Off

Laure generously gives me a whole month to recover but she says—through Marcia—that she expects me to be in top form when I return. She hired a couple of new apprentices because word about the restaurant is continuing to spread and it's busier than ever.

At the end of my second week at home, Marcia invites me for coffee on a Tuesday when the restaurant is closed. She picks me up in her car at my parents' house and we go to her favorite coffeehouse, not too far from the restaurant.

She grills me for details about the stabbing, and she gossips about the new apprentices, who are both having a hard time keeping up with the pace of the restaurant.

Marcia says, "I bet Laure will kick out at least one of them when you return. I miss you, you know. Can't wait for you to come back."

"I'll be back in two weeks. I hope my shoulders won't be sore by then."

"Good," she says distractedly, her gaze drifting up to someone behind me. Her lips break into her brightest smile and she says, "Come join us."

I crane my neck to see who can bring that extra sparkle on her face. Leon smiles down at me. My breath catches for a second or two but seeing him reminds me of Cristi. I scowl, annoyed that he stands next to my bench, clearly expecting to sit next to me. I don't budge and I glare at Marcia.

Leon says, "Not Marcia's fault. I badgered and bribed her for this meeting."

I don't look up and I don't move.

Marcia gets up, reaches over to pat my hand. "Don't be too mad at me. And hear him out. He means to make up for what happened."

To Leon, she says, "I'll do a little shopping at the boutique next door. I'll be back in half an hour."

Leon sits where Marcia sat. He says, "You don't know how sorry I am for what you had to go through. I suspected something was wrong after my chauffeur came back a few times unable to deliver your flowers. He said no one seemed to be at home. So, I called Marcia. She told me about the stabbing."

I'm still annoyed at Leon, but now, also at Marcia. I feel like she deceived me. "You know Marcia well enough to call her?"

He smiles. "Marcia and I go back a long way. Before she started working at Laure's restaurant. I don't know why she didn't tell you."

"Was she one of your conquests?"

"You are direct, but I like that. I'm not one to kiss and tell, though. You'll have to ask Marcia. I'll respect what she decides to share with you."

I shrug. "She probably was, then. Doesn't mean anything to me. Well, I don't mean to be part of that unfortunate group."

"Not all of them in that group will agree with that assessment, I assure you."

"Maybe not. Anyway, your attention is wasted on me. I've already been hurt by it. I don't intend to suffer from it more than I already have."

"Okay, I can accept that. But won't you let me make up for it?"

"I don't need you to make up for it and I don't see how you can. I've lost a childhood friend because of you."

"That's not really my fault, though, is it? It certainly isn't something I'd have wanted to happen. Have you thought about the possibility that Cristi just has a fragile ego?"

"I won't listen to you badmouth my friend."

"No, I'm not badmouthing her. I just want you to see that you can't really blame me for something Cristi did."

"Okay, I won't. But Cristi doesn't deserve to spend time in prison. She was in pain and wasn't thinking when she attacked me. So, no, you're not responsible for her attacking me, but you did hurt her."

"For that, I'm truly sorry. I thought she understood that I couldn't promise her commitment. I made that clear when we started going out."

"I don't know what Cristi understood. But I know she was suffering. And I think you're so self-centered, you ignored what you call her fragile ego."

Leon winces and he's turning red. "Is that what you think of me? A selfish bastard?"

I don't answer. Maybe, I've offended Leon enough that he'll leave. I didn't mean to, but I'm still upset at what happened to Cristi.

But Leon doesn't leave. He says, "You're right. It's a mistake going out with Cristi. Actually, I broke up with her once I realized she was too fragile. But, apparently it was too late."

Leon surprises me. I didn't think he was capable of seeing—much less of admitting—he'd made a mistake. I say, "Please let's leave it at that. I want to move on, that's all, and for me to do so, I'd like you to turn your attention somewhere else." I start to get up but he reaches out and restrains my arm.

"I want to move on, too. Get beyond that unfortunate incident."

"Good. Then we agree. Let's start by you letting go of my arm."

"I'm in love with you, Gina. I don't see how I can move on without me telling you that."

I'm dumbfounded and, for the moment, I can't move a muscle. I never expected such an admission. I can feel my heart flutter. With excitement, yes. Pleasure? That, too, for sure. I'll be lying if I say that a declaration from a guy like Leon doesn't get to me in any way. The fact is, it does. Big time. Still, there's Cristi. Who knows how many more Cristis there have been among Leon's conquests?

As tempted as I am to find out what it's like for Leon to love me, I tell myself that it can only end in heartache. So, finally, I say, "You'll get over it. It can't be anything meaningful. You hardly know me. Anyway, you've had a lot of experience getting over things, after all."

"You mean my attraction to your friend Cristi?"

"And Marcia and God knows how many more women out there."

I try to get up to leave, but I'm flabbergasted to find my legs have turned to jelly. Leon's "confession of love" must have affected me more than I realize.

Before I can think of what to do, Leon says, "You're different, Gina. I've never fallen for anyone the first time I met them."

"It's lust, not love."

"Maybe, but the women, I've been with—they fall for me before I fall for them. Cristi included. My trouble is, I can't resist the allure of a pretty woman. When you think about it, they seduce me. And, maybe that's why I tire of them eventually."

I think *How can they not?* but I say, "That sounds like a lot of ego to me—to think that women seduce you."

"They do, actually, in so many different, individual ways. You did, too, but effortlessly. Maybe just by being who you are. The others are pretty blatant about their attempts. But I fell for you even before you became aware I was there."

"Lust, I still say. Anyway I knew you were there. As I was leaving the kitchen Marcia warned me that "Table 29 guy" was a regular client Laure wanted to keep. But at the time, I was more anxious that the dish I was serving would make a good impression. It's basically my creation that Laure and Guy worked on with me."

"I sincerely loved your tuna, and I told Laure so."

"Thank you. That means a lot to me."

"I think you have a promising future as a chef."

"You think so?"

"I'm considered a connoisseur of good food, as you might know, so you can take my word for it."

"I love experimenting with new dishes and I'd love to open my own restaurant but that may remain a pipe dream."

"Who knows? Anyway, Laure also thinks you have great potential. That's quite an endorsement coming from her. I know she'll help you as much as she can. So, you must hang on to your dreams."

"I mean to. I'm really just starting, so you could say I'm still burning with hope."

He smiles. "I'll hang on to mine as well."

"I bet you don't have to worry about making your dreams come true."

"Why? Because I was born rolling in dough? True, money has gotten me farther than anyone I know and I don't think I'd ever want to be without it. But it seems my money is not enough to get me everything I want."

"Then I guess you can take your own advice and hang on to your dreams. They may come true someday."

"Don't you want to know what my dream is?"

"Not particularly. But if it makes you feel better to tell me, go ahead."

"Mine is for you to give me a chance, one day, to show you I can make you happy."

I blush and say nothing.

Leon says, "Do you think my dream will ever come true?"

I stay silent a little while longer. Leon watches me, and waits.

I'm getting more uneasy. Finally, I say, "I'm open to being friends. You seem nice enough."

He smiles doubtfully. "I'm glad you at least feel that way. I'm friends with Marcia. But I don't think that's possible between you and me. I'm sure, sooner or later, I'll try to make love to you."

"Then it looks like we'll have to say goodbye right here, right now."

He smiles ruefully and gets up. "Here comes Marcia, but I promise you this isn't goodbye. I don't give up easily."

Leon is gone before I see Marcia coming from behind.

She sits down at the place Leon vacated. She looks contrite. "I'm sorry to spring that on you. But he kept hounding me. Then he bribed me." She takes out a package she's obviously bought at the expensive boutique she went to.

She opens it to show me a beautiful necklace, studded with what I'm sure are diamonds. "I'm such a sucker for these things. This is something I can never afford on my salary. Well, maybe I could, but I'd have to work years to save money to get this. But it's peanuts to Leon. Will you forgive me?"

I can't help smiling. "Oh, Marcia, what am I supposed to say? With Cristi hating me now, you're the only best friend I've got. And how can I deny you something that seems to make you so happy? Well, it's not me who gave it to you, but I guess I helped in some way."

"You sure did. If not for you, Leon would never have thought of bribing me."

Chapter Ten

Back to Work

On my first day back at Du Cœur, my senses come alive again at being with people who work hard and take pride in creating dishes that not only give our customers pleasure but also new dining experiences. Inventive concoctions they won't easily forget; feasts for the eyes, nose and taste buds. That's the wonderful thing about being at this restaurant. I didn't realize how much I missed it.

I also find, though, that after a month of near idleness, not only does your body get flabby and lazy, your skills can rust. So for a few days after I return, I come in an hour earlier than usual. I do some prep work to get used to the feel of the knives, the pans—all the various "tools of the trade" so that I can go about my tasks without having to think about them.

I want to live up to Laure's opinion of me. I'm also banking on what Leon said about Laure helping me go after my dreams.

I haven't seen Leon since the coffee shop and he has stopped sending me flowers. I am relieved but also a little sad. Regardless of Leon's effect on me, those roses brightened my days and my drab, cramped apartment. I miss them.

My life is back to its normal, hectic routine—I find that comforting. Nothing much out of the ordinary to upset me or excite me too much. I can focus on working toward the day I can take full charge of my life; when it's me who decides and chooses what I need to help me get what I want. For now, all I have is a dream. The dream my grandfather started. He's communicating with me, Mom says. He wants me to finish his dream.

The restaurant opens for the week on a Wednesday and it's the start of my third week back. It's past four in the afternoon and in an hour, the first customers will be arriving. The pace in the restaurant has picked up. The arms in my muscles are tense and beads of sweat are flowing down my neck and my back.

I'm startled from my concentration on the fish I've been slicing by Laure's voice. She's standing behind me. "There's a Lieutenant Hansen waiting to talk to you in my office."

"But ..." I protest, gesturing towards the filet of fish.

"Go! I'll take over what you're doing until you come back."

I wipe my hands on my apron. I'm a little irritated at getting my work interrupted, so I don't care if Lieutenant Hansen thinks I smell fishy.

Like the first time he came to ask me for my version of what happened with Cristi, Lieutenant Hansen plays the polite and formal detective. He gets up, greets me, and shakes my hand.

Our eyes meet and for a few moments, neither of us speaks. I smile shyly, and find myself apologizing for something I thought I didn't care about. "My hand's fishy. I'm sorry."

He gives me a little smile. "I've smelled worse." He has a nice smile although it doesn't lift the troubled look in his eyes. "This place smells delicious, though."

His gaze flits from my face down to my toes. "And white suits you."

Warmth creeps up my face; I must be blushing. The sad solemn lieutenant has taken the edge off my irritation. He can appreciate good things, after all.

I take the seat across from him. "We're lucky. We get to smell what's cooking, and we also get to taste it."

"It must be wonderful to work in a place where what you do nourishes both body and spirit in your customers."

He understands what my work means to me and I smile sweetly, ready to answer all his questions. "What can I do for you today, lieutenant?"

"First, I thought you should hear this from me. The district attorney is filing a battery charge against Miss Silva."

"Oh, no! Does that mean she'll go to prison?"

"That's possible, but you never know how a jury will go. The max for a prison sentence for battery is two years but she could get out before that."

"I'm so sorry for Cristi. Even a day in prison will be bad for her. She really doesn't belong there. Is there any way I can help so my testimony would make it easier on her?"

"You'll have to talk to a criminal lawyer. You have a big role in this trial, Miss Lambert. You're the prosecution's main witness."

"How do I talk to a lawyer? I don't even know where to find one."

"A lawyer from the DA's office will likely talk to you, but he may not be the right person to ask. His intent is to convict. The defense lawyer will probably talk to you, too. She's the one to ask. She's a no-nonsense but very helpful lawyer."

"You know who'll be defending Cristi?"

"I've heard rumors. Nothing has been announced. Miss Silva's family can't afford to hire a lawyer so someone from the public defender's office has been assigned to defend her. I do still have a couple of questions to ask you, Miss Lambert."

"Call me Gina, please, unless you're not allowed to."

The shadow of a smile plays on his lips again but he ignores my remark. "How well do you know Leon Barrett?" He sounds like a teacher asking questions on a history or literature exam.

"I've actually only talked to him twice."

"When?"

"I already told you about the first time—I served him and Cristi a dish I created here at the restaurant."

"You mean when he was on a date with Miss Silva?"

"Yes"

"Did they come back together for dinner?"

"No; not together. But Mr. Barrett has. He's a regular."

"Was he alone or with someone else?

"I think with someone else. With his family once, for sure. Other times he came with another man or another woman."

"Did you talk to him those other times?"

I shake my head.

"When was the second time you talked to him?"

"About a month ago, at a coffee shop."

"A couple of weeks after the stabbing incident. Was that a date?" Up to this point, the lieutenant has kept his deadpan face. But this time, I notice a flicker in his eyes; a flicker, maybe of greater interest.

His question irritates me, though. "No, I didn't even know he was going to be there. My friend Marcia, the pastry chef here, arranged it without telling me."

I proceed to tell him more about the meeting at the coffee shop, again in as much detail as I can remember. I make it clear that I told Leon to turn his attention elsewhere. I don't know why but I wanted the lieutenant to understand that.

When I finish, I say, "Will they have to call him as a witness?"

The lieutenant ignores my question. "He's been sending you flowers for weeks but you've only really talked once."

His remark irritates me all over again. "I've no time to see anyone. This work keeps me very busy and often exhausted. Who knows—maybe Mr. Barrett's family owns flower shops."

"You never asked him to stop?"

"Stop what?"

"The flowers."

"I was going to but Marcia said not to bother so long as I didn't take them seriously. She knows him quite well, you see. So, I just let them come, thinking he'd soon get tired sending them. Besides, they're really nice. I don't get too many nice things like that."

"Did you tell Miss Silva about the flowers?"

"I didn't have to. It seems Mr. Barrett told her about them. She says that's also how he let her know he was interested in her."

"How many times did he have to send them before Miss Silva agreed to go out with him?

"You have to ask Cristi but I think not many at all."

"Hmm," he says and, unexpectedly, he answers the question which he previously ignored. "The DA decides if he needs Leon Barrett as a witness to argue his case. I think he'd rather not bring him into this if he could help it. Mr. Barrett isn't a stranger to these proceedings. He was in a case like this three years ago. Normally, these cases don't hit the papers but he's from old money, handsome, pursued by many women; so there was more press attention than is usual for such cases. The DA wants to prevent the media feeding frenzy that came with that trial."

"Never heard of the trial. Too busy. When I get home, all I can think of is sleep. What's it about, anyway?"

"Mr. Barrett, as you may know, is known to run around with quite a lot of women, most of them not from rich families but working women. This particular young woman stabbed herself in the stomach and claimed he did it. As in Miss Silva's case, Leon Barrett had broken up with her. Her motive, though, was revenge. It went nowhere. Some evidence didn't add up. Plus her lawyer was no match for what the Barretts could buy. She later admitted she lied. The case was dismissed."

"That's dumb—getting revenge that way. She could have died."

Lieutenant Hansen says, his eyes clouded by his knitted brow. "She could have. Luckily, she didn't. She sustained a fairly serious injury. But I've seen worse things. Much worse. You never know what people can do in desperation.

He gets up and extends his hand. "Thank you again for answering my questions." Then, he leaves the room.

I follow him out the door, wondering what "worse" things Lieutenant Hansen has seen in his job. He intrigues me in a way quite different from the way Leon does. It must be those eyes that speak of a tortured soul he can't hide even when he smiles, which I've only seen him do twice. I get a strange urge to turn him around, kiss that sadness out of his eyes.

As if he read my thoughts, he turns toward me and gives me an unexpectedly bright smile. "It's been a pleasure meeting you, Regine. Maybe, we'll meet again under happier circumstances."

Before I can reply, he's briskly walking away and out the door of the restaurant. I smile and say to myself, "I'd like that, Lieutenant Hansen."

Why he called me Regine, I can't say. I've always insisted on being called Gina.

Chapter Eleven

Persistence

My hope that Leon won't bother me again is dashed the following Tuesday. I'm getting ready to go home to my parents when the bell rings. I look through the peephole in my door and I see red. Nothing but red. I'm tempted to pretend I'm not home because I know what it means. But my curiosity gets the better of me. Besides, those flowers are beautiful.

So, I open the door and Leon's chauffeur hands me a huge bouquet of red roses and thrusts an envelope in my hand. This time, the roses exude a heady whiff of fragrance.

But I shake my head. "Take them back, please. Tell Mr. Barrett no offense, but I can't accept them."

The chauffeur says, "My instructions are to leave them by your door no matter what. I think it's best to take them, Miss. It'll be such a waste. These roses are so beautiful and so fragrant."

I relent a little. "I'll have the roses, but not the envelope."

"I told you, my instructions are to leave them by the door, flowers <u>and</u> envelope. Why not just accept it, Miss? You don't have to read it."

"You're right," I say as I snatch the envelope from his hand and tear it and its contents to pieces. "There. Now you can tell your master you delivered both flowers and envelope."

The chauffeur says, "I don't think it's a good idea to tear it, Miss."

"It's been given to me. It's mine so I can do as I please with it," I say, grinning at him.

He shrugs and adds, "Yeah, but I know Leon. Ah well! See you again tomorrow, Miss Lambert."

He means it. On Wednesday morning a few minutes before I leave for work, the doorbell rings and I see red through the peephole. Again. The chauffeur grins and says, "Good morning, Miss Lambert. Good to see you again." He thrusts flowers and envelope at me, gives me a slight bow, and turns on his heels.

Since then, he's been flashing that amused grin at me, the same time, day after day. My actions don't vary: I scowl at him, take the flowers and shred the envelope in the same dramatic fashion.

A week later, I decide all that drama is lost on the dutiful, loyal chauffeur. So, I say thank you and take both flowers and envelope. Until the following Tuesday.

When he hands me both, the chauffeur says, "Leon says he'll stop sending these if you read the letter."

"But how does he know I'm not reading the letter?"

"Don't know, Miss. Why don't you just read it? Maybe something in it'll tell you how come he knows you're not reading it."

"Okay," I say, feeling defeated. "I just want him to stop bugging me."

The letter is handwritten. I didn't expect that.

It's actually pretty touching, knowing that he took the time and effort to write me a letter by hand. Who does that anymore?

As I begin to read, I can't help wondering if this particular letter says the same thing previous ones did. For a moment, regret nips at me. I'll never know what's in those earlier letters since I threw them away as soon as I closed the door on the chauffeur.

In the letter, Leon says he's staying away on the advice of his lawyer. And he'll stay away until the battery charge against Cristi is either resolved in court or settled. Like me, he thinks she doesn't belong in prison. Maybe, we can work together to help her.

He wants to do what he can, short of paying for her defense, which will only attract needless attention. In any case, Cristi is getting Elise Thorpe, a smart lawyer from the public defender's office,—a lady well-versed on women's issues.

If I agree to work together, I should call his lawyer. We'll talk only through him. Leon leaves a phone number.

I can't think of a reason not to work with Leon to help Cristi through his lawyer; so I dial the number.

"Hello," a familiar voice answers.

Even on the telephone, I'd recognize that voice. I'm puzzled and I hesitate, but I also become aware that my heart is thumping louder in my chest and my hand is clutching my cell phone tighter.

"Gina, please don't hang up," Leon says.

"You tricked me. Like that time at the coffeehouse with you and Marcia."

"Forgive me. I just wanted to hear your voice. It will be a long time before I hear it again."

"Does this lawyer even exist?"

"He does, actually. I can give you his name if you really want to know."

"Not really. Will you stop sending me those flowers, then?"

"Yes. Scout's honor."

"Good. I'll hold you to it."

"May I say one more thing before you hang up?"

"What?"

In a tender voice, he says, "I want you to know I can be patient. For me, this whole Cristi affair doesn't change anything. I'm still in love with you."

I should remind Leon that I don't want to get involved, but I'm at a loss for words. He does make my chest flutter. And how often does someone like me attract a man like him?

Leon is not really my idea of the type of man who excites me. To me, Lieutenant Hansen is that man—tall like Leon, lean but taut with muscles beneath his shirt, strong features that reflect torments you can't even guess at, especially in his eyes. He intrigues me. I want to look deep into his soul, but I'm afraid he won't make that easy. Leon is beautiful, with fine features and the polished air of someone who's been catered to all his life. You don't have to look too deeply to know what he is. He doesn't belong in my world. But Leon also knows exactly what to say. How to say it. And when.

Leon is waiting for me to speak. Matching his gentle tone, I say, "What am I supposed to say, Leon? I've no control over how you feel."

"I don't expect you to say anything. Not now. I just wanted you to know. Goodbye for now, my sweet dream." He hangs up and the excitement in my body slowly ebbs into disappointment.

I wonder: Am I capable of what Marcia half-jokingly suggested—go out with Leon, have fun, and don't expect anything more serious. Then, I'll never have to wonder again what it's like dating someone rich and sophisticated, someone like no one I've ever met.

Chapter Twelve

Marcia

Marcia nudges my arm. I'm slicing golden beets for a salad we're serving as first course in this evening's tasting menu. "Come on, let's go take a break. I'm dying from the heat in here."

"Go, then. Don't wait for me. I'll join you in a few minutes."

"No. I know how you can forget time when you're working. A few minutes to you can mean a half hour. Come on. I need company. Those beets are done, anyway."

I put the beets in a bowl, rinse my hands and wipe them on my apron. I follow Marcia out the back door. She sits at one end of a pile of empty crates we've turned upside down.

"Give me a minute. I'd like to return a call I got about an hour ago."

"Who from?" Marcia says.

"Cristi's lawyer, I think, from the contact info."

I call the number; a recording answers. I leave a message about a good time to call me back.

"No answer?" Marcia says.

I shake my head as I sit next to her. I stretch my legs out, a position I find relaxing.

"Have you met her yet?"

"No." I scowl, feeling weary of Cristi's problems. "Let's talk about something else."

Marcia points to a couple of girls walking by, headphones in their ears and cell phones in their hands. "I think you and I are the only ones who come out to relax here without those thingies in our ears."

"Most people like to relax to music," I say.

"No, that's not it. They tune out, like those girls are tuning out, not only from the world around them, but also from each other. I think those thingies are their way of telling others not to bother them. People are such pathetic loners. I'm a pathetic loner."

"But you and I have each other. We're very good friends and we talk. Not like those two."

"You're a pathetic loner, too. We talk, but only during break. The only time you and I did something together outside these breaks was when I set you up with Leon. Deviously, I admit."

"This work keeps us too busy, or too tired for anything else."

"That's what I mean." Marcia heaves a sigh, long and deep, and deliberately dramatic. "I need something else in my life."

"Don't you have other friends?"

"Not here. In Oregon, yes. Did I tell you I left a boyfriend there to work for Laure here?"

"No. What was he like?"

"Sweet, real sweet. But he married a former rival three months after I left. I think he became too lonely. Maybe he was getting back at me for leaving."

We're both silent, sobered by how our choices have plunged us into pathetic loneliness. Marcia turns to me. "I need a replacement. Can you introduce me to that brooding detective who came here a couple of weeks ago? He looks like he can use some loving; some of my pastries, too."

"You saw him?"

"Yeah, nosy friend that I am. My cakes were in the oven; so I peeked in on you in Laure's office."

"I didn't see you."

"No, you couldn't. You two seemed deep in conversation. You wouldn't have budged if someone shouted 'fire.'"

"Well, he was asking questions and I needed to jog my memory to answer him truthfully."

"Was that it? You looked more like lovers having an intimate conversation," she says, her eyes twinkling with mischief.

I shake my head in protest. "It's those chairs by Laure's desk. They're placed right next to each other." I'm conscious of how lame my explanation sounds. Am I denying what she seems to be implying because there's a seed of truth in it? With the detective's long legs, we were sitting knee-to-knee. I gave him my full attention and I'm quite sure he gave me his.

"That's it, I'm sure, those chairs." She gives the hand on my lap a gentle squeeze. "Anyway, if you choose Leon over this brooding hunk, can you introduce me to him?"

"But how? The detective and I aren't friends, not even acquaintances. I see him only when he has questions to ask me for his investigation."

"I'll come up with a plan. How about you invent an excuse to see him in his office and I go with you?"

"But what excuse?"

"I'll help you think of something."

Frowning, I say, "You think Lieutenant Hansen is attractive? He's a bit rough around the edges."

"Honey, that's part of what makes him hot. The other is his brooding face. That mouth! I could swallow that lower lip whole. Slightly open from disgust; or could it be from suffering? I'd like to know what's going on in that head of his."

"You just might have the chance if you come up with another devious plan."

"Oh yes, I'm a master of devious machinations. I'm not planning one, though."

I smile but I'm uneasy.

Marcia says, "You still have a lot to work out, don't you? The haute cuisine trade can gobble you up, and Cristi's case is a bitch. Isn't she getting on your nerves?"

I chuckle, "Yes. The case is getting tiresome."

"For me, too. Do you sometimes wish you could see Leon, talk to him?"

"Not really. Out of sight, out of mind, I guess. He does make my heart go thump, thump when I see him. He's quite delicious to look at."

"He is that, especially with all that moolah. But you're keeping things cool. Bravo! That way, you don't get your heart broken."

That evening, as I'm sinking into sleep, I mull over my conversation with Marcia. Her probing, telescopic gaze misses very little. And she's frank, at least with those she counts as friends. It's a precious trait in a friend you confide in, like I do in Marcia. I prefer the truth to lies, even when truth is devastating. Lies meant to protect me can actually hurt in the end.

I've disclosed my innermost thoughts to Marcia and she knows the big and little scrapes I've gotten myself into. But have I been honest enough with her? How honest can you be with another if you're not honest with yourself first? Like everyone else, I have doubts and I don't always get why I act the way I do. Or, maybe, I know why but I refuse to see it.

What did Marcia expect me to tell her about Leon or Lieutenant Hansen? And how can she be attracted to the detective when they haven't talked at all? True, her keen eyes saw his brooding nature right away. But she says it's his mouth. I say it's those clouded eyes, and "brooding" does describe them.

The detective. He's never revealed his first name. But I would have liked to know it. When I remember those two times we've talked, I'm filled with a kind of warmth that I've felt only in intimate conversations with Mom, Sabine, or Adam.

I can see myself loving him. Maybe I do already. Is that the truth I can't disclose? A truth I can't admit because it makes me feel naked? To Marcia, anyway. I doubt the lieutenant has any interest in me except as the victim of one of his cases. So I don't worry about him knowing. But Marcia is on to something. An unspoken connection. A connection she grasped when she saw the lieutenant and me in Laure's office.

What about Leon? I can't ignore him. I doubt he'll let me. And it puzzles me that I also find him attractive.

*****

I wake up the following morning to dusky light diffused by the dusty, blue curtains that came with the apartment I'm renting. The night seems to have crept by without my noticing it. Much like the way my electric-light days inside Du Cœur's kitchen flash by me unnoticed, until I close the restaurant door behind me to face the black night again.

It's Sunday but I have to work. I drag myself out of bed, hobble a few steps to the window, part the curtains for the bright southern light, and raise my face to the sun, my eyes closed. It's a ritual I do every morning.

Heat and light from the sun warms my body, sharpens my senses. I open the window wide and the faraway drone of the morning commute turns into a racket of cars revving up, whizzing by or screeching to a stop, punctuated by an occasional blast of a horn or someone cursing. But the racket helps. It assures me I am where I want to be.

These mornings, I've been more relaxed. I don't get twitchy anticipating the doorbell minutes before I leave for work. Yes, I miss Leon's roses, I even miss the chauffeur who used to deliver them. But losing those roses is the price I've gladly paid for a tranquil existence. Now, I can focus on working—without distraction—to make my dreams come true. And after I remind myself it's not just my dream, but my grandfather's as well, I've harnessed all the energy I need to begin my day.

I am, at core, a pessimist. Sometimes when I'm being kinder to myself, I say I'm practical. I don't believe in planning for a future that includes another person, unless I know for sure that person wants to be a part of my life. But I also realize we can never tell what's going to happen tomorrow. Or next week, or the week after that.

Since I've returned to my absorbing, exhausting routine, I haven't been back to visit my family, which is how it has always been. Lately, though, Mom has been calling more often. I think that, ironically, the stabbing incident has brought her and me closer. It took a little tragic incident for us to start talking more openly to each other.

In the past, weeks can pass by when we never hear each other's voice. These days, she calls Tuesday nights. Sometimes, she calls twice a week. Often they're "how-are-things-going" calls that last five minutes, but occasionally they stretch to a half hour when one of us brings up the subject of food and cooking. She's genuinely interested in the dishes I prepare at the restaurant and I find she has a deep knowledge of food, earned through experience.

It's those long conversations that have drawn us closer. Without having to say "I love you," she's shown me how much she really cares for me, for all her children. Now I realize that she prepares her special meals not so much because she loves cooking, but because it's her way of showing us how much she cares.

Chapter Thirteen

Coffee Break

Can I get you something to drink? A cup of coffee, soda, water?" the receptionist says as I sit on one of four chairs around a round table in a small room.

"No, thank you," I say.

"Attorney Thorpe should be here shortly." She smiles—a practiced, mechanical smile—and closes the door.

Lawyers intimidate me, though I can't say why. It doesn't help that this room is so small and I feel trapped in it. It's quiet, with touches to make visitors feel not so cooped up and isolated within the small space. A pot of healthy violets in the center of the table. A wall of glass windows shared with the office hallway. But I still find it oppressive. Maybe it's because I don't know what to expect.

I've formed a murky impression of defense lawyers from television: People in dark suits who try to confuse and break down witnesses whose testimonies might be working against their client. But Cristi's lawyer is a woman; maybe she'll be sympathetic, especially if I tell her I'm not here to make Cristi pay for what she did. Maybe she won't attempt to confuse me.

In the middle of that last thought, the door opens and a very pretty blonde woman in red suit enters, carrying an olive green folder. I like red. I don't have any dark associations to it like I do with all shades of gray. She smiles at me, reaches over to shake my hand. She can't be more than five years older than me. She says, "Ms. Lambert, how do you do? I'm Elise Thorpe. I'll be defending your friend Cristina Silva."

"I'm fine. How do you do Miss Thorpe?" I take her offered hand and notice the diamond ring on her third finger. She grips my hand firmly, ignoring my mistake in addressing her "Miss." I begin to relax a little, although I can't help wondering how one so young can have the experience to prevent Cristi from going to prison. Do I also feel some envy? I wouldn't have studied law if I had gone to college, though I wished what I did was as noble as defending another person's rights, like this lawyer is doing.

She sits across from me, opens the folder, and leans forward. "Thank you for coming. I'll be recording this interview. Will that bother you?"

"No, not at all."

She doesn't attempt small talk. She says, "Ms. Lambert, you've been friends with Cristina since childhood. How close were you?"

"Very close. We shared our secrets. We were also neighbors so we came and went into each other's house every day."

"Did you have any fights, misunderstandings, times when you felt so angry that you hated the other?"

"We had misunderstandings, but not fights, and I surely don't hate Cristi, never hated her."

"Do you think she'd say the same about you?"

"Say what about me?"

"That she, Cristi, doesn't hate you, has never hated you."

The question catches me off guard and I stare at her with my mouth open. I never thought about it before, but at the moment, I can't say for sure that Cristi doesn't hate me. "I honestly don't know. Cristi is so sweet, so mild-mannered, I can't see her hating anyone."

"Is there any reason you can think of for her to be so angry with you to the point of hating you?"

I stare at the table. No one in our parents' neighborhood knows much about Cristi's two former boyfriends and her accusations that I lured them away from her. Was she so angry at me those two times that she actually hated me? "Well, maybe," I say.

"So, what might that reason be?"

"She had a couple of guys who turned their attention to me, who broke up with her. But we were just teenagers then."

"Can you remember how old you were at the time of those boyfriends?"

"The first one was when I was fifteen, at the end of my first year in senior high. She was two years ahead of me. The second one was three years later, the year I graduated."

"How did Cristi take the breakups?"

"For the first one, she came to my house, accused me of stealing her boyfriend. Then she ran out of the house and refused to talk to me for a few months. She did pretty much the same thing for her second guy, although she actually burst into tears before running out. Both times, though, she never raised her voice, just had this hurt look in her eyes."

"Did you and Cristi make up, become friends again? Who made the first move to reconcile?"

"She did. Both times. I wasn't mad at her. I stayed away because she ignored me when I tried to patch things up."

"Is Leon Barrett the third boyfriend she's accused you of stealing?"

"Seems so. But I never hooked up with either of those first two guys, and I told Mr. Barrett he's wasting his time on me. The second one tried to make up with her but she wouldn't take him back. Mrs. Thorpe, if it's going to help Cristi at all, I want you to know I don't hate Cristi, even after she tried to stab me. I think she was distraught and wasn't thinking right. I don't think she should spend time in prison. I don't want her to go to prison. I think she'll go crazy in there."

"You'd say that even after she went at you with a pair of scissors?"

"She didn't mean to. I think she grabbed the first thing she could lay her hands on to strike me with. So, yes, I'm sure she was quite mad. She had this crazy glassy-eyed look when she raised her hand for the second time, as if the real Cristi was not there. I felt somehow that she didn't know who I was, that she wasn't aware of what she was doing."

"Are you prepared to say all that you've told me in court, Ms. Lambert? All the things you just told me are not in any of the reports I've read."

"Of course, I am. No one has asked me the questions you've asked. And I never thought to tell anyone. Do you think my testimony will help her?"

She leans back on her chair. "It certainly will, especially since it's consistent with the psych report by the psychologist who saw her shortly after she was taken into custody." She pauses and fixes her gaze thoughtfully on me. "You and Cristi are friends and you seem to be sincerely anxious to see that she doesn't go to prison."

I nod. "I'm anxious about her. I think what she needs is help."

Elise Thorpe leans forward again. Her lips twitch into the beginning of a smile. "Ms. Lambert, I'll do what I can to have the court dismiss the case against Cristi. Your testimony today will help that. If that fails, then, I'll work toward a plea bargain that she can accept. That means the case won't go to trial but she might be put on probation. I'll argue for psychological counseling. If that still doesn't work out, we'll go for an NGRI plea— that means 'not guilty by reason of insanity.' She won't go to prison but she'll likely be required to go to some facility for psychiatric care. She needs that right now, anyway, since she's suffering from severe depression according to the results of the psychological workup by our psychologist."

"Thank you for telling me all that. That reassures me that Cristi is in very good hands. You've also given me a better impression of lawyers." I wanted to add, at least, of you in particular. But I decide it's more appropriate to end with a smile. I like her. She respected my intelligence by sharing her strategy and not sparing me the legal terms.

"You're quite a lady yourself, Ms. Lambert, standing by a friend. I think it's brave and it shows integrity."

Before I leave, she extends a hand to me again. We shake each other's hand more vigorously, although that's probably me shaking hers a little longer out of gratitude. This interview has eased my anxiety, lessened any guilt that still bothers me about Cristi.

She says, "I hear you're a chef at Du Cœur. I've only been to that restaurant once. My husband prefers intimate dinners at home when we celebrate ..."—she laughs—"anything, really. Your restaurant serves great food. Inventive dishes, but tasty and a feast for the senses."

I smile, embarrassed. "I'm just a cook and it's not my restaurant."

She smiles—a casual, reassuring smile. "Well, I bet you want to own one someday. I wish you much luck and when you do have your own place, send me an announcement."

*****

A couple of months later, I get a call from Lieutenant Hansen. "Miss Lambert, I thought you might like to know. You'll get an official notice from the

DA's office but I thought I'd spare you a few days of anxiety. Miss Silva isn't going to trial. Seems like her defense lawyer negotiated a favorable plea bargain for your friend."

"Thank you, lieutenant. That's such a relief. And how nice of you to inform me as soon as you knew."

"My pleasure, Miss Lambert ... Gina. At some point, the district attorney will probably inform you of the terms of the plea bargain. Conditions she's accepted, like probation and going to therapy."

"Thank you again." I hesitate. We're at the point where I should hang up. But I remember Marcia's request. "Lieutenant Hansen ..."

"Yes, Gina? Anything else I can do for you?"

"No, nothing ... I think. Well, yes, there is but I don't know if it's appropriate." An idea has suddenly hit me.

"Tell me and I can tell you if it's allowed." I can almost hear a smile of amusement in his voice.

"I'm aware you've been assigned to ... interrogate me—is that the word? I think it's my turn to tell you how much I appreciate the fact that you've been so considerate and shown such concern every time you asked me questions. I don't know if other detectives are like you. Anyway, I wanted to know if you might join a couple of my friends and me for dinner one evening. My way of giving thanks."

"That sounds real tempting. You cook for the best restaurant in the area so you must be exceptional. I've never totally forgotten those delicious smells that day I came to badger you with more questions. When is it going to be?"

"I haven't a firm date yet. I'm still waiting for my friend to confirm. Can I call you back on it?"

"Sure. You have my card. Use the second number. Thank you. I've always wondered what it's like eating at that restaurant."

"Well, I won't be preparing anything as fancy. But I'll try to recreate a dish or two we serve there."

A few days later, an official looking letter arrives from the district attorney's office. A resolution has been met in Cristi Silva's case and there won't be a trial. Cristi won't be going to prison. She has agreed to psychiatric care at a state-funded facility where she'll stay two months.

Just like that, it's over. I'm relieved. But also sad. I think I've lost a childhood friend.

But it's time to move on.

*****

I have a new problem. Well, it's not exactly a problem. At least I don't think so but it will take time and effort above my usual routine. I have set myself up for giving a dinner. How do I do it in my cramped, ugly apartment? In a kitchen with tableware for two, a saucepan, a skillet, an electric hotpot, a ladle, and a spatula. And a razor-sharp chef's knife.

On my next break with Marcia, I bring up the matter of the dinner with Lieutenant Hansen.

"Marcia," I say. "I'm in a bind and you're mixed up in it."

"Tell me. I might be able to fix it."

"You have to because Lieutenant Hansen is mixed up in it, too."

She grins broadly, "Well, well. Definitely count me in."

"Then, you're invited to dinner with the lieutenant and another friend I don't have."

I recount my conversation with Lieutenant Hansen, starting with his news about the closing of Cristi's criminal case.

She says, "Great! Not a moment too soon. It seemed like you put a good part of your life on hold."

"Yeah, sometimes I think I must have felt guilty for Cristi's attacking me."

"You mean like it's your fault."

"Yeah, like I drove her to it."

"No, you didn't and I won't go into the usual clichés to convince you it's not your fault. The whole unfortunate episode is over. Done with. *Finis*. Move on."

She slaps her hand lightly on my thigh. "Anything I can do for that dinner besides dessert?"

"Okay, moving on. The problem is, I committed to this dinner but my apartment is cramped and, frankly, I'm ashamed of it."

"Consider that problem solved. We'll do it in my big, well-appointed—by me, that is—condo. After all, you're doing this for me and the lieutenant. What's problem number two?"

"The 'other friend.' The one I don't have."

"What about Leon? Duh!"

"I don't want to involve him in this."

"Come on, Gina. Cristi is history. Live a little. Have fun. Leon will give you that and more, I assure you."

"I've asked him to turn his attention elsewhere. If I invite him he'll think I didn't mean what I said."

"So what? That's the great thing about being a woman. Men think we're fickle so we can change our minds anytime we damn well please. Take advantage of your advantages, woman."

"But what if Lieutenant Hansen and Leon are uncomfortable with each other? Lieutenant Hansen has investigated another case before that involved Leon. Maybe those two can't stand each other."

With a mischievous twinkle in her eye, Marcia says, "That'll give them something to talk about. Anyway, I'll take care of the lieutenant if you take care of Leon. They may not have to interact much with each other at all. I have two bedrooms, you know."

"Marcia, you're naughty. That wasn't part of my scheme. This is a get-acquainted dinner."

"Gina, this is the twenty-first century, the era of quick bytes and fast forwards. I want to get past the intro as quick as possible. But more to the point, my clock is ticking way too fast for me."

"You think the lieutenant is husband material?" The idea of the lieutenant being married to Marcia gives me a queasy stomach.

"I haven't thought that far ahead. But I wouldn't mind making a baby with him." Once again, that mischievous glint in her eye. And that queasiness in my stomach.

"Break is up," I say, looking at my watch and getting up. I trudge ahead of Marcia through the back door into the kitchen.

*****

I call Lieutenant Hansen on my way home from the restaurant. It's a business number, and I intend to leave him a message. But it isn't a machine that answers.

"Hello, Miss Lambert ... Gina."

Surprised, I say, "Hello, Lieutenant, are you still at work?"

"No, I'm at home."

"I'm sorry. Did I wake you up?"

"Actually, I was just about to go to bed."

"I thought this was your work number."

"It's my personal cellphone. I only give it to a few people."

The lieutenant's answer gives me pause. I don't quite know what to make of it, but I smile, pleased.

"Am I one of the few because I'm inviting you to dinner?"

"I gave you that card before you invited me."

For an instant, I'm speechless and the lieutenant says, "What's up? Anything I can do for you?"

"Yeah. About that dinner? Two Mondays from today. Can you make it? Sorry it's your work day, but that's when the restaurant is closed."

"I'll be there. Where?"

"At Marcia's place. She's my friend. Pastry chef at Du Cœur." A little uneasy anticipating the lieutenant's reaction, I add, "I think she's inviting Mr. Barrett."

But Lieutenant Hansen doesn't hesitate. "Sounds good. I'm looking forward to it. Where's Marcia's place?"

"Can I email it to you tomorrow?"

"I don't usually check my email at home. Can you write it on a piece of paper? I'll pick it up at your work."

"Isn't that more of a hassle than checking your email?"

"Not sure. The thing is I forgot my password." He pauses for an instant. "How about I come take you out for coffee tomorrow? Your day-off, right? Kind of like a pre-dinner thank you. And my coffee break."

"I'd like that," I say.

The turn of this phone call doesn't exactly fit my image of the formal, business-like Lieutenant. But it suits me much better.

I open the door to the Lieutenant at ten o'clock in the morning. Same jacket, blue jeans, sad eyes, and deadpan face.

"Good morning, Lieutenant," I say, stepping out and closing the door behind me. "Shall we go?"

"Good morning, Regine." His serious face gives way to a smile. "You put a smile on my face."

I smile back, quietly surprised that his face can actually light up.

I'm wearing flat sandals and he seems taller. Neither of us says anything until we're in his car. "There's a place in Emeryville I like to go to. Is that okay?"

"Sure if it's not too much out of your way."

"No. Anyway, I need to get away from work now and then. I'm back to doing homicide cases."

"That doesn't sound like fun."

He shakes his head, frowning. "It's my job."

The serious face is back and I can't think of anything to say. But strangely, I feel okay being quiet. Usually, with people I'm just getting to know, I find silences awkward.

The coffeehouse is cavernous. A banquette lines a long wall. We claim the only empty table on a corner by the wall-length window. Except for the low drone of conversations at a couple of tables, it's quiet and no music plays in the background.

Minutes later, we sit side-by-side on the banquette. We're having large lattes. Lieutenant Hansen asked for whipped cream on his low-fat latte. Mine has soy milk.

I wait, amused, while he takes his first sip, scooping a good amount of the melting whipped cream with it. He says, "Whipped cream is my one indulgence."

I nod, handing him the piece of paper with Marcia's address.

He licks his upper lip before he takes the paper. "Thanks."

After entering the address and phone number on his cell phone, he tears the paper into pieces and says,

"First name is Brent, Regine. That's what friends call me."

"I got used to calling you lieutenant."

He grins. "I guess I have to bug you more, give you practice to say Brent."

"Okay. Brent. But why Regine?"

"Suits you better. Something a bit exotic about you."

"I'm a quarter Chinese, a quarter French."

The hour or so we pass at the coffeehouse puts me in a happy mood. But I realize later that, though he gave me a lighter version of Brent Hansen, he told me nothing more about himself than that he has an older sister with fraternal twins and his parents live in Oregon.

Chapter Fourteen

Four for Dinner

Marcia convinces me we should invite Leon to be the fourth person at the dinner, but I'm hesitant to ask him myself. So she volunteers to call him.

Leon is in Paris when Marcia calls. But he'll be back the evening of the dinner to which he will surely come, although he may arrive a few minutes later than the designated hour.

The day before the dinner, I call Lieutenant Hansen.

"Regine. What can I do for you? I'm salivating just thinking about tomorrow's dinner."

"I hope you won't be disappointed."

"I know I won't be. How often does one get invited to dinner by two chefs from the best restaurant in the city?"

"Marcia is a pastry chef. I'm just a line cook."

"Same difference to me. Anyway, can I help?"

"Can I hitch a ride with you to Marcia's place? Save us both a bit of gas. I can buy you a tankful."

"It'll be a pleasure. But I won't accept the gas. Remember, you're giving me free dinner."

"Thank you, Lieutenant Hansen."

"Brent, Gina, remember? Lieutenant Hansen across a dinner table sounds a bit formal, don't you think?"

"Okay. Brent, can we go half hour earlier?"

"That can be arranged. How about I pick you up at seven?

Brent Hansen rings my doorbell at precisely seven the next night, a bouquet of white roses in his hand. He's wearing the same dark suit jacket. But tonight, he has paired it with a beige shirt and well-pressed navy pants. No blue jeans. At my eye level, dark hair on his chest peeks from the opening on his shirt.

I look up, a little embarrassed. Did he catch me staring at his chest? "Hello Brent. Come in. Let me just finish packing the main dish."

"Hello, Regine," he says. The amused smile he's trying to suppress tells me he did see me staring. He hands me the roses.

"Thank you. They smell so good."

"You're welcome. I've got another bouquet in my car for your friend."

"Can you wait a couple of minutes?

"Anything I can do to help?"

"No, I'm almost done. I'll just put these in a vase and finish packing my dish."

Ten minutes later, we're approaching the Bay Bridge to San Francisco. Neither of us has said much beyond, "Nice night, isn't it?"

He casts a quick sideway glance at me. "I hope you don't mind my saying how beautiful you look."

"No, I don't mind. Thanks. You look good yourself."

"Thank you. I don't often take these pants out of my closet. I live in denim most of the time. It's rugged and easy for moving and poking around in. You never know what you'll get into in a crime scene."

"It must be hard investigating assault and battery cases."

"For me, it often is. I usually handle more serious cases."

"You mean murder?

"Yes. Cristi's case was a little break I asked for."

"Do you get many—murder cases, I mean?"

"Yes, more often than I'd care to, but that's my job. This county has more than its share of killings." He scowls, and the serious detective is back.

"Is that why you have this sad look in your eyes?"

"Do I?" His scowl deepens.

"I think you know you do."

He's silent through the rest of the drive on the bridge.

"I'm so sorry. Did I offend you by what I said?"

"No, oh no. I actually thought you're very perceptive. Nobody has ever said anything about my 'sad eyes.'"

"You've got them, though."

"We're trained not to get emotionally involved in our cases. But when you see so many dead victims and how they died … the anguish of their friends and relatives—that's harder than anyone cares to admit. So, yeah, my cases depress me. But my real problem has to do with understanding why people kill. I don't just mean the motives a perpetrator confesses to. Or the motive for killing a lawyer proves in court. And I do understand that opportunity can make it easier to kill. Homicides are high in this country because guns are easy to get. Studies have shown that time and again. Anyway, it's hard to explain. It's a philosophical question, not a moral one."

I fight the urge to touch him, to tell him that, though I can't grasp the "philosophical question" he's grappling with, I can sympathize with how he feels.

"Philosophical questions may be above my head. But I understand moral concerns. What you've seen in your job, I can't even imagine. I think most killings are senseless. I've sometimes wondered if humans are violent by nature. And I agree it's so depressing that killings happen."

"I'm so glad you understand. It means a lot to me."

I rarely tell people about the murder of my grandfather. It's not a secret, but it's too personal to share with just anyone. Somehow, I don't feel that way with Brent.

"I do know firsthand that a killing can ruin the lives of loved ones victims leave behind. And those consequences can be felt by future generations. My grandfather—my mother's father—was murdered."

The lieutenant jerks his head towards me. He clenches his jaw, and scowls once again. "Oh Regine, I'm so sorry."

"It happened before I was born. Mom was nine. She saw him in a pool of blood. I'm sure she suffered the most.

"But it's not just the anguish. Much of that fades with time. For Mom, I think what's been most harmful is she lost her desire to dream. She was caught up too young, coping with the day-to-day realities of losing her father. And we've felt the effect of that—she couldn't teach us how to dream, either. Mine is a loving family,"

I pause, frowning. "But we're content to remain white trash."

Brent is silent. What can he say, after all? I glance at him. His frown has deepened and his shoulders droop. Like someone carrying the weight of the world on his shoulders.

Neither of us says any more until we arrive at Marcia's condo. He says, "You're not white trash. Look where you are. You must have talent to cook for that restaurant."

"Thank you, Brent. We can park on Marcia's driveway."

He nods. I open the passenger door but before I can step out, he grasps my hand, "Gina ... ."

Our eyes lock, but it's through his hand on mine that I sense something like electricity pass between us.

It takes him a minute full of unuttered words—words with meanings I can only guess at—before he speaks. "Thank you for inviting me. I'm sure I'll never forget this evening, Regine."

He brings my hand to his lips and grazes it with a light kiss. My hand twitches as if it's reacting to a matchstick ignited next to it, itches where his lips touched it. I withdraw my hand from his grasp.

Conscious that we can't meet Marcia while still in the grip of that "electricity;" I say blithely, "My pleasure. It isn't as if you and I are on a date. It's a dinner for us to get better acquainted, that's all." In my head and my guts, I am excited, bewildered, happy.

Marcia opens the door before we reach it. She beams at me, then at the lieutenant. "I saw you both from my bedroom window. Come on in."

Once inside, I introduce Brent to Marcia. Brent offers her a bouquet of yellow roses before he shakes her free hand. Marcia leads him to the couch, and though I want to stay, I excuse myself. It's what Marcia expects—we have planned this dinner so she can meet the lieutenant. "You two can get acquainted. I'll finish this dish in the kitchen."

Before I go, Marcia says, "The smoked salmon you ordered is on the second shelf of the refrigerator. And Leon called to say he's on his way. He'll be here in fifteen minutes."

I nod, and glance surreptitiously at the lieutenant. He seems unconcerned at the mention of Leon but I sense that he's avoiding my eyes.

I'm still in the kitchen when the doorbell rings and Leon comes in. I hear him greet Marcia warmly. Then he says, "Lieutenant Hansen, what a nice surprise to see you here."

"So you know each other?" Marcia says with feigned surprise.

"Quite well, in fact. Wouldn't you say, Lieutenant? Although, the lieutenant knows me much more than I know him."

Brent says, "Yes, you could say that. I got to ask all the questions. A lot of them. I guess this is your chance to ask, if you care to get to know me better."

"I'll take you up on that. You've always intrigued me, especially when someone told me you have a law degree from Boalt Hall. We're both Cal Berkeley alumni. Why do police work when you can make more money lawyering? Those credentials can get you anything you want."

"Meting justice starts with good police work. I decided when I graduated that I want to be at the beginning of the process."

"I can't agree with you more on the ties between police work and justice. Marcia, I owe this guy here. He asked all the right questions and did such thorough investigation that I got a false charge dropped."

Marcia says, "I know the case. Had more media coverage than it deserved. I didn't know Brent was the investigator in charge of it."

"Brent! Is that your first name? May I call you that, too? Have you two known each other long?"

Marcia says, "No, we only met today."

"Oh! You looked so cozy together, I thought ... where's Gina, anyway? Is she here?"

Brent says, "She's in the kitchen."

"I'll go see her. Brent, I look forward to talking to you more."

Only a wall separates Marcia's kitchen from her living room and the door between them is open so I heard the whole conversation among the three of them. In the two or three minutes Leon and Brent talked, I found out more about Brent than he's ever told me in the twenty-minute ride from my apartment to this place, or in the few short conversations we've had on the phone or in person. And yet, those are mere facts. There' so much more about Brent that I think I know, but you can't list them like you list facts.

I hear Leon's footsteps coming closer and my grip on the ladle tightens. Am I excited to see him again or am I dreading it?

"Gina, there you are. I've missed you so much."

I put the ladle on a spoon rest on the counter and face him. "Hello, Leon."

Leon is scrutinizing me with his sticky gaze. "You look like heaven this evening. I've only seen you in white chef jacket or, once, in blue jeans. You're stunning in royal blue."

I ignore his compliments. "How was Paris?"

"Magical, as always. I'll take you there sometime. I was mostly in meetings with clients, representing my father, so I didn't get to see much of the city this time around. Anyway, I think, it'll be much more fun when you come with me."

"But who says I'll go with you?"

He smiles gently. "You will eventually because I won't stop asking until you say yes. That really looks good. May I taste it?"

"Sure," I say, handing him a fork.

Leon takes a piece, chews it slowly. "It's delicious. I can see it's chicken but what did you put in it? Nothing like I've had before."

"That's because you've only eaten at fancy restaurants. This is good old home cooking. A recipe from my mother. I do have a fancy first course."

"So what's your secret ingredient? Mustard, maybe?"

"You've got a good nose; good taste buds, too. It's the best Dijon mustard I could buy."

"Finished with heavy cream?"

"What else? My mother is half French."

"But what are these black bits floating on top?"

"My mother is also half Chinese. They're chopped up black mushrooms. It's an experiment. You all have to tell me if it works. Do you cook?"

"Not really. But Luciano often asks me to taste test dishes."

"Oh, yeah, I forgot. You have servants and a cook."

He chuckles, "He's okay. Not as creative as you, though."

Marcia and Brent have joined us in the kitchen and they're standing on either side of Leon.

Marcia says, "Let's eat. You're making Brent and me hungry. I set the dining table before you all got here."

Leon says, "Good idea. I usually don't eat the meals they give you in plane trips, although Air France has better food than most. So I'm starving."

I say, "Can we make this all very casual? I want a break from all the ceremony we put clients through at Du Cœur."

Marcia says, "Hear, hear. But we shouldn't skimp on good wine. So where's the wine, Leon? You're usually my supplier."

"Sorry, Marcia. I didn't have time to get wine. Shall I call my driver to get us a couple of bottles?"

I say, "No, please. I saw a few bottles of wine in Marcia's pantry. I'm sure those will do."

Leon addresses Marcia. "Have you drunk the merlot I gave you last time I was here?

I cast a curious glance at Marcia, then at Leon. They know each other more than they've let on. "No, that'll work. I also have a couple of bottles of Riesling."

The dinner is pleasant and noisy, more so as three of the four of us get more drunk. After the first glass of Riesling, Lieutenant Hansen refuses Leon's offer of more wine with a simple, "I'm driving."

Although he's the only one who has stayed sober enough to remember what he's saying, Brent doesn't say much until Leon prods him.

"Brent, you promised to even the score by answering all the questions I ask you."

"Did I say that?"

"I thought so. But anyway, here's what I've been dying to know about you. We all want a truthful answer. Do you have a life? I mean you're so dedicated to your work. Do you ever leave it at the office and do something you're passionate about?"

Marcia and I stare at the lieutenant with round eyes, barely able to disguise our curiosity. I'm sure he'll dodge the question and give a vague answer. I decided early on that Lieutenant Hansen is a very private person, slow to share all but trivial details about himself.

But he surprises me. He answers without hesitating. "I don't really have one. Not outside my work anyway. I'm single and my time is my own. It may sound trite or pompous, but my passion is for truth and justice. So I'm where I want to be, doing what I want to do."

"No girlfriend?" Marcia says.

"No, not at the moment. But I don't want to talk about that, if you don't mind."

Marcia grins. In a self-satisfied way, I think. "Fine by me."

Leon says, "I'm not sure if your answer satisfies me. I think you're evading my question."

Brent says, "You asked for truthful. I gave you a truthful answer."

"Aren't you afraid you're missing something?"

"Like what? Excitement? There's a whole lot of adrenaline you can get in my job, although for me, adrenaline kicks in from the process of solving a crime. Much of the rest of it can be gruesome, which I'm sure people would be glad not to have in their lives."

"What about the finer things in life?"

"I'm here now, enjoying some of the finest things with you."

"I bet this is rare, though."

"Of course, it is. How often do you have two chefs from the best restaurant cook for you? Actually, my sister is also a good cook, and I usually have dinner at her house on Fridays."

"I still think you're evading my question."

Marcia gets up. "Leave it, Leon. Anyone for dessert?"

Leon says, "You know my answer to that. What do you have?"

"Gina said not to make anything too fancy. So I have goat cheese cake and fresh raspberries, with or without crème Chantilly—your choice."

"I'll have raspberries, please. A touch of crème Chantilly," Brent says. "No goat cheese cake."

"Why?" Marcia says, frowning and looking dismayed. "Is it the goat cheese? Don't you like it?"

"I like goat cheese; but except for fruit, I don't eat desserts. It's the sugar."

"But I make a great goat cheese cake. Ask Gina."

"I'm sure you do. But I have diabetes in my family."

"Sugar doesn't cause diabetes."

Marcia is still unhappy, so I say, "Marcia, let's respect the lieutenant's choice. Between Leon and me alone, we'll gobble up your cake."

Leon says, "Gina is right, Marcia. I know you're quite proud of your goat cheese cake. But not everyone likes or can eat dessert."

She turns towards her kitchen, mumbling, "How can anyone not like dessert?"

I say, "Can I help you with the dessert?"

She answers by tilting her head toward the kitchen.

In the kitchen, I watch Marcia take out a carton of whipping cream from the refrigerator. "What's that all about, Marcia?"

She doesn't answer. She's scowling as she pours cream in a bowl, adds a swish of Grand Marnier and some powdered sugar, and turns on her mixer.

As she's transferring the whipped cream into a pretty bowl, Marcia says, her scowl deepening, "How can I hook up with someone who doesn't like my desserts? I love what I do, damn it. I want the person I live with to eat and love the product of my efforts."

"Oh, Marcia, I'm sorry." I begin to laugh.

"What's so funny? I'm serious."

"I know you are, but are you going to let something like that get in the way of what you want? Isn't what you have between you and the one you love more important?"

"He's not the one yet. Anyway, making pastries is part of who I am. How can someone know and appreciate me if he has no understanding of what I do?"

"I see. I'm sorry I laughed. I guess I was separating what you do for a living from who you are."

"You can't. Anyway, forget it. Let's bring these to the table. I know Leon will like them." She picks up the tray of goat cheese cake and whipped cream, and hands me the bowl of raspberries.

"I'm getting the sense that you and Leon know each other a lot more than you've let on."

"Don't go there, Gina. Not now. If you want, we can have a confessional later, just you and me."

Leon and I go "ooh-aah" every few bites of the goat cheese cake, and praise the raspberries. Brent relishes his plate of berries, licking whipped cream off his lips. Marcia is uncharacteristically quiet.

Not too long after dessert, Leon says, "I'm afraid I have to call it a night. Jet lag. Work, too, tomorrow."

He turns to me. "May I take you home, beautiful?"

"I came with Brent. I'll go back with him."

"Oh! All right. I'll call you sometime soon."

I don't answer him. I start to stack up the dishes on the dinner table.

Brent says, "I'll do it, Gina. You cooked. Marcia, can you show me where your dishwasher is?"

As if awakening from a nap, Marcia gets up to help Brent, then leads him toward the kitchen. I watch them with a nip of jealousy.

Leon says, "This was wonderful, Gina. Thank you for inviting me. Marcia said you hesitated to do that."

"I thought it would be awkward. Not only between us after that afternoon at the coffee shop, but between you and the lieutenant."

"I feel very much at ease with you, and you needn't have worried about Brent and me. I like him. A whole lot. He's a straight shooter. I'd like to be friends with him but we move in different social spheres." Leon pauses an instant, then he adds, chuckling. "And who knows? Sometime in the future he may have to investigate another incident I am allegedly—I think that's the word they use—involved in. If that happens, we'll both need some distance between us."

I smile at him. Maybe Leon is kinder, more considerate than I thought. I may have let gossip and events of the last few weeks taint how I see him. Tonight, all he's said, all he's done, have chipped away at the wall I've tried to build between us.

The ride back across the bridge to the East Bay is as pleasant as the earlier one to San Francisco. But Brent Hansen is quieter this time, almost as uncommunicative as he was the first time he came to ask me questions about the stabbing. I lean my head on the head rest. I'm drunk, I think, and I doze off. Sometime later, I hear Lieutenant Hansen call my name.

"Regine, Gina, we're here."

I open my eyes to gaze into his melancholy ones. Before I realize what I'm doing, my hand is touching his cheek. He places his hand on mine, peers into my eyes. I think he's going to kiss me. I wait, my heart thumping so strongly I wonder if he can hear it.

He lifts my hand off his cheek and up to his lips. He kisses the palm of my hand, his lips lingering on it, his breath moistening the skin around it. I gasp. It's the sweetest kiss anyone has ever given me. A kiss that seems to come from deep within. A kiss that tells me a lot about Brent. It's a moment that will keep haunting me.

He raises his head, smiles, and with my hand still in his and resting on his chest, he says, "I'll take you up to your apartment. You're a little drunk."

I nod in agreement. He gets out of the car, comes to my side to open the door, and helps me out. He puts an arm around my shoulder and I lean on him, clinging on his arm. I think, at that moment: It's the place I'd like to be, enclosed in Brent's warmth, reassured by his strong, steady arm around me.

He says good night after I open the door to my apartment and abruptly turns to walk away. I watch as his back recedes and disappears down the stairway.

"Stay with me," I say to the oppressive air in the empty hallway.

Chapter Fifteen

A Quick Lunch

I slip the eye mask off my eyes and over the top of my head. I put it on at night when I don't have to go to work the following day.

Soft blue light, filtering through the dusty blue curtains, floods my bed. Outside, it's a bright sunny morning but I can't budge my body off the bed. Maybe I can stay a little longer and get more sleep. I pick up my cell phone from the bedside table and look at the time. Eleven in the morning. What is there for me to rush to? It's Monday, a week after the dinner at Marcia's apartment.

An extra half hour might be enough to wake my body up slowly. I close my eyes again. But not long after, the chores I have to do for the day scroll down my mind's eye like the closing credits in a movie. I blink to zap the screen in my mind. Poof! Gone. But just as I'm dozing off, the film credits play again, large and white and defiant on a black background: *Wash your underwear, iron your chef's jacket, vacuum the dust off the curtains, go to the grocery ...*

Only one way to kill the pesky words for good, I'm afraid. I open my eyes to the diffused blue light on the apartment wall directly in front of me; at least it's not black. Goodbye pesky white words. But—hello chores. There's always a price to pay.

I slide my slug of a body into sitting position. I'm sitting, but why does it feel like I left my brain on the pillow? The slug plops back down to reconnect with my brain and curls up into a fetal position.

Jolted from stupor by the ringing of my cell phone, I kick my legs straight out from my curled body. It's a half hour past noon. My brain, it seems, halted to a stop without informing me. For a whole hour, at least.

The number is one I vaguely recognize.

"Good afternoon, my love."

"Leon," is all I can say. My brain is not in gear yet.

"Have you had lunch? What if I buy you one? I know a food truck with great hamburgers that will be parked today a mere couple of miles from where you live."

The mention of food wakes up my stomach. "You eat out of food trucks? Isn't that too ... too pedestrian for you?"

"Not this one. Anyway, ambience is important to me only for dinner. At lunch, if the food is fresh and well-prepared, I'll bite. Literally."

It's tempting but I hesitate. How about my resolve to stay at arm's length?

"Come on, Gina. It isn't a date. Just two food lovers seeking out food. You might learn something from this guy. He's into fusion. How do Korean-style hamburgers sound to you?"

A lunch of my favorite smoothie of bottled Mango Tango, crackers, and cheese? Or kimchi on a beef patty? The choice is clear for me. Plus Marcia's words echo in my awakening brain. *Take advantage of your advantages, woman!*

"Okay. Half an hour?"

"I'll pick you up."

"There's fire in them burgers," I say after my first bite of a grass-fed beef patty adorned with pickled cabbage smothered in garlic, green onions and red chilies.

I take a gulp of my sparkling mineral water. Leon is having a small glass of wine with his kimchi burger. Who knew food trucks offered wine? But the food in this truck isn't your run-of-the-mill offering. The burger is organic ground chuck.

He says, "Does the strong aroma of kimchi bother you?"

"Are you kidding? Some French cheeses can beat this sucker for fragrance anytime. I like it. Garlicky, spicy, stinky."

"Great," he says, chomping on his burger.

We eat in silence for a while. He bought his driver, Will—the thin man who has been bringing me the roses—American-style hamburgers, Asian fries (dipped in a soy-based sauce) and a bottle of beer. He's sitting next to Leon, wordlessly finishing off his two burgers.

"Does it bother you? The smell of kimchi?" I ask Will.

"I was born and raised in a small town in Iowa, Miss Lambert. Pig town. But I'm too old for those"—he points his chin at my burger—"and stinky French cheeses."

Leon chuckles, "Sometimes he has no choice, though. I've dragged him to places where he can't get his American hamburger."

"So, what's the worst lunch Leon has forced on you?"

"Fried squid. The rings aren't so bad. But they mixed in these pieces with little tentacles." Will crinkles his nose and shudders in distaste.

Leon and I can't help laughing.

I note that Will seems to enjoy dipping his fries in the soy-based sauce. "That's not like in Iowa, though, is it?"

Will says, "I like soy sauce. Even in Iowa, we had Chinese restaurants. This is good. Wanna try it?"

I shake my head. "No thank you. I've had fries with soy sauce."

Leon has finished his lunch. "I have to get back to the office. Meeting at two. How about we have lunch together on your days off, explore these little places that serve good food? I've scoped a few of them out."

"Sure," I say without thinking, without bothering myself with the thought that I'm being inconsistent. I'm discovering little facets of Leon that appeal to me. He isn't the snob I thought he was. And he seems to have a sense of adventure.

"Pick you up same time tomorrow?"

For an instant, I'm dumbfounded. Is that what this means? Leon and I (and Will, most likely) lunching together twice a week, except when he has some other commitment? Maybe I agreed too quickly. And yet, I did have a very pleasant lunch. One I'd choose again over bottled organic Mango Tango, cheese, and tomatoes while scrolling or reading my cell phone screen in my pajamas.

I say, "Sounds good."

And that's how I begin to see Leon twice a week. Maybe it's a clever ploy on his part, a strategy that will lead to "Have dinner with me?"

A few days later, the doorbell rings and through the peephole, I see white. All white. This can't be Will the driver. I can't imagine Leon sending me or anyone else white roses. White doesn't mix well with drama.

It isn't Will. A young man in short sleeves with a florist logo on his shirt says, "Good morning. Is this the residence of Miss Regine Lambert?"

"Yes?"

"Flowers for you, Ma'am." He hands me the roses, mumbles "Goodbye, Miss," and runs down the stairs.

The flowers are from Brent Hansen, with a card tucked among the roses:

I've been meaning to call you. Thank you for the best dinner I've ever had. I'm working on a new case— a hard case—and it has kept me very busy.

I offer a peace offering for taking this long to thank you. I hope you like it.

Think of me sometimes, Regine.

Think of me sometimes, Regine. How deceptive these words can be. To me, at this moment, they speak of endings, not beginnings. Memories, not fresh adventures. Do you mean to say goodbye to me, Brent

Hansen? Does your passion for truth and justice exclude someone like me? Will you at least be thinking of me?

The card that came with Brent's roses puts me in a gloomy mood while I'm getting dressed for work. But an hour later, the sight of Du Cœur makes me smile. It's going to be another busy, exciting, exhausting day.

An hour before customers arrive, Marcia and I take a break. We're once again sitting on the turned-over wood crates; taking simultaneous swigs from our bottles of water. My bottle is half-frozen and the first sip I take is a shock to my throat. It takes me some seconds before I take another. I stop drinking only when the content is down to the ice.

Marcia frowns. She has been watching me, her eyes amused. "Boy, are you thirsty, kid. What have you been up to?"

"To tell the truth, for the last two weeks I've been going out to lunch with Will and Leon on our days off. We're sampling all kinds of places for eating. I guess I've been having too much kimchi and soy sauce lately."

"Wait...wait. Are you saying Leon has finally gotten to you? And who's Will and what's kimchi?"

I grin. "Is Leon getting to me? Maybe. He's fun, that's for sure. Not the food snob I thought he was."

"That's great. Truly glad. Now I won't have to feel so guilty about that diamond necklace. But how did this all come about?"

"Well, Leon called one day. Quick lunch, he says. Not a date. But what really got me was the kimchi burger."

"Kimchi?"

"Korean pickled cabbage. Spicy stuff. Anyway, he says he knows other little places, most of them ethnic. It's been fun trying them out and I'm getting ideas for dishes. We've only had one misadventure so far."

"Which is?"

"A place that serves raw chicken. Just couldn't get into that."

Marcia makes a face. "Ugh. Me neither."

I chuckle. "Will actually refused to come in with us. He went looking for a hamburger joint."

"Who's Will? Sounds like your chaperone."

"Will is Leon's driver. Nice man in his fifties. I think Leon used to drag him to these places. Now he's taking two of us."

"Leon does know how to have fun. I envy you. Now, if I can only get him to give a bit of that love for fun to Brent."

I shake my head a little. "Brent sounds too busy for anything but work."

She nods, "I sent him a text message the other day. To say hello."

"You've forgiven him for the goat cheese cake. Good for you."

Marcia chuckles. "Not exactly. I've decided he's not my type. It isn't just the goat cheese cake. He's a bit too intense, too serious for my comfort."

"He believes in what he does. Like you do. But he deals with death, you deal with pleasure."

"It's kinda chilling the way you put it: 'He deals with death.'"

"But that's what it takes, doesn't it? Being a homicide detective. I'm sure it's tough. Might make you lose faith in humanity."

"But as they say, someone's gotta do it. Anyway, knowing Brent made me realize I prefer my men easygoing and laid back. I don't think I'll want to listen to accounts of shooting and butchering before we make love. Can't do it. Too depressing," Marcia says, with an exaggerated shudder.

"Most people wouldn't, I think. Maybe, Brent knows that and that's why he's got no girlfriend or wife."

"You've thought about this, haven't you? Sometimes I forget I have more than ten years of experience on you."

I take what she said as a compliment. "No. Just thought of it when you said he was too intense, too serious."

"Do you like him?" Marcia is regarding me closely.

I return her intent gaze. "I do. Despite what you call his brooding nature. He's well put together, has things under control, and tries to do right by everyone. That's reassuring."

"I wouldn't mind a few good laughs with him. Do you think he has a sense of humor?"

"If one is serious by nature, does it mean he can't tell when something is funny or silly or ridiculous?"

Marcia laughs. "Watch it, kid. Don't go philosophical on me. That's nearly as grim as talking about dead bodies. Anyway, all I'm aiming for is a roll in the hay from time to time with the intense lieutenant."

"Then I guess I have no more to say."

Marcia grins. "One thing I got right, now that I've seen him up close. He's awfully sexy and he doesn't seem to be aware of it. It makes him even more irresistible."

I smile wickedly. "If Brent is as intense about what you call 'a roll in the hay' as he is about his job, you're in for a real treat."

"I expect him to be. And it'll be a big blast. But he hasn't answered my message yet. Well, he did, but only to say he was busy on a new case and would text me again later."

"Why don't you just ask him out?"

"Actually, I did. Invited him to dinner at my place. Just the two of us. No desserts, I assured him. I have recipes from my mother, too, that men I dated before Brent have raved over."

Chapter Sixteen

Sushi

Will stops in front of the modest-looking restaurant Leon has chosen on this Tuesday, the fourth week of our lunches. Leon waits outside the door, holding the doorknob. I'm partway in, surveying the noisy crowd, most of whom are students at the nearby university.

Will says, "If you don't mind, I'll go for a burrito. There's a Mexican place down the street. I don't like fish. Never had raw fish, and never will."

Leon grins, amused. "You sure? You don't know what you're missing. You can order tempura or teriyaki. There's soy sauce in the teriyaki."

Will shakes his head. "I think I'll pass."

Leon and I join a small line ordering at the counter. He says, "This place is usually packed at noon. The crowd is thinning out so we'll have a quieter lunch."

"You've been here before."

"A few times. For a small mom-and-pop place, the sushi here is quite good. People know it and they come. I hope you like sushi."

"I've only had it twice. I never ate at restaurants when I was growing up. Unless you think McDonald's and Wendy's count as restaurants. That's all my family could afford, and not often. I had sushi at a popular Japanese restaurant with an old boyfriend."

"Was he a sushi eater?"

"No. He ordered chicken teriyaki. I had sushi."

"Then, I suggest you try their rolls. You'll like them. You can graduate to nigiri later. That's a slice of raw fish on top of rice."

"I'm not squeamish about raw fish. We use a lot of it at Du Cœur, as you know. And I'll take sashimi over beef carpaccio or steak tartare anytime. What would you suggest in nigiri?"

"Would you trust me to order for us?"

I nod since Leon obviously knows more about sushi than I do.

Fifteen minutes later, a young Asian waiter places a large platter with an assortment of sushi on the table. With his chopsticks, Leon picks up a piece from a row of rolled sushi topped with tiny orange fish eggs. He reaches across the table to offer it to me.

Surprised by his gesture—which seems so intimate to me—I hesitate at first. He's watching me; smiling, waiting, expectant. The expression on his face is one

I've seen on my youngest brother when he offered Mom a frog in a jar he caught from our garden.

I open my mouth for the piece of sushi. It's a mouthful. I bite into briny eggs which burst in my mouth, sinking into the tangy, salty-sweet blend of soft rice, seaweed, cucumber, raw fish, wasabi, and mayonnaise. Leon is watching my reaction.

"Great stuff, wonderful combination," I say.

He smiles, gives me a thumbs up, and picks up a piece for himself.

Halfway through our plate of sushi, I say, "Next time, let's go to a place that serves dim sum."

"Yeah let's. I've never been to one. I do have a pretty good idea what it is. It's like a Chinese version of small plates."

"Better than that. You get so many more choices."

"Do you know a good place?"

"There's a good one by the bay in Emeryville. I went there once with my ex-boyfriend."

Leon nods before he picks up another piece of sushi. He's silent as he devours three more pieces. Then, he glances at me and says, "What happened to him?"

"Who?"

"Your boyfriend."

"Oh, him. He proposed and I turned him down. I've never seen him since."

"Why? Fell out of love with him?"

I shrug. "No. I was nineteen when he told me he loved me. A year later, he asked me to marry him. I always thought I'd say yes. But at the very moment he popped the question, I had a vision of myself shriveling into an old hag before I was forty. Shriveling while my family grew fatter and older."

Leon laughed. "Funny imagery. Anyway, I think twenty is too young to be tied down to a family."

By the time we finish the whole plate, it's two o'clock and only four other customers are left, all sitting at the bar.

"Don't you have to hurry back to your office? I wonder what's happened to Will."

"He went home. I'll take you back to your apartment."

I look at Leon suspiciously. "Did you arrange all this?

"I wanted to be alone with you. Is that okay?"

I smile. "Yes. It's been nice—these past four weeks."

"Will you have dinner with me, then?"

I giggle and cover my mouth with my hand.

"What's so funny?"

"I knew we were going in that direction. I wondered how long it was gonna take before you ask."

"Would you have come after the first week?"

"No. Not the second week either. You've been patient and I appreciate that."

"I didn't want to rush things. I wanted you to see I'm not the ass people say I am. Those people don't know me."

"But you don't deny you're a playboy?"

"I've played around. I think everyone should. And no one should marry until after thirty. Or until they outgrow playing around."

I say wryly, "So, you're living true to your convictions."

"I won't deny it. Did you love your boyfriend?"

Caught off-guard, I frown. Leon has had a habit of bringing up new or tired topics when I least expected it. Maybe it was his way of shifting conversation away from himself.

Annoyed, I say, "That's none of your business, is it?"

"No, you're right. I'm sorry. So, will you go out with me?"

I don't answer right away. Leon waits, peering at my face. "God, you're beautiful. I've never seen anyone quite like you before."

I'm used to Leon's little seduction tricks by now. He's trying to mollify my annoyance but I can't help smiling. "Okay. But let's go somewhere not too fancy. Something like this, but a little more formal."

He gives me a glowing smile. He actually looks pleased. "I'll be violating my dining ethics, but for you, I'll do it."

*****

Late that night, my phone rings. I pick it up as I lie in bed reading, waiting for sleep to come. Another little surprise. This time, from someone who I believe to be so thoughtful and considerate that he won't bother anyone past ten in the evening. If it had been Leon calling, I wouldn't have answered. But it's Brent.

He says, "I'm sorry to be calling this time of night, but I know you keep late hours. How are you doing?"

"You didn't call at midnight just to ask me that."

"I did, in fact. It seems to be the only time I have for myself lately. I've been thinking a lot about you since that dinner at Marcia's."

He pauses, but not long enough for me to answer. I can't speak, and the hand holding my phone has begun to shake.

"I feel bad, guilty that I didn't call you or at least send a thank you card soon after the dinner."

I sigh. Is that the only reason he's been thinking about me? "Don't worry about it, Brent. You did send me roses. That makes up for anything you think you failed to do."

"You liked them, I hope." He has an unfamiliar tremor in his voice; a shakiness I've seen in someone losing control.

"I loved them. Is anything wrong? You sound different."

"I'm tired, that's all. Things are becoming so complicated."

"Your new case?"

"It's not that new anymore. But that's not all of it."

"You care to talk about it?"

"I can't. Besides, I don't want to bother you any more than I already have. You've got work tomorrow. I hope someday I can tell you more. It's good to hear your voice, though. I'm feeling better already."

"My voice doesn't have that much power, does it?" I say, teasing. "But I'm glad I can make you feel better. I like hearing your voice, too. It makes me feel good."

Brent takes a moment to speak and he ignores what I said. "Well, I should say goodnight. Long day again tomorrow. Yours and mine. Goodnight, my child."

I protest. "My child? You can't be that much older than me." Actually, what I want to say is Don't go. Not yet. I want to hear your voice a little while longer.

"No, seven years isn't that far apart. Good night, Regine." He pauses and sings a short phrase from an old song. "I'll see you in my dreams." He has a good singing voice and he can keep a tune. I want to tell him so but he hangs up.

I get up from bed. I'm too restless. Brent's call is a jolt I didn't expect.

I swipe my book off the bed and take a few paces to my refrigerator for the only bottle of wine in my apartment. It stands among shorter plastic bottles of sparkling water.

With half a glass of white wine in my hand, I sit on my armchair and open the book on my lap. I start to read but I can't concentrate. Brent's face seems to be staring at me from every page of the book I turn to. Looming behind his face is Marcia's.

That night, I dream I'm running after them. They look back, laughing at me. The face on Marcia's body changes to that of Cristi as she runs. Then, she stops, looking like Marcia again. She stretches her arms to block my way. Laughing louder, she strikes me with a chef's knife and I stare at Cristi's face once more. I struggle to wake up gasping for breath.

Chapter Seventeen

Dinner with Leon

On Sunday, after the last customers leave the restaurant, Laure approaches as close as she can get, and whispers that I can take the next Sunday off. I didn't ask for it, so I stare at her, puzzled. She's not letting go of me, is she?

Maybe, she senses the panic rising from my gut because she chuckles and shakes her head, assures me it has nothing to do with my work. That, in fact, I've become a very valuable part of her team; that I'm doing even better than she expected.

But I must still look bewildered. She pats my arm and lowers her voice again. "I'm doing it as a favor to Leon."

I should have guessed.

The next day, at lunch with Leon, I try not to slurp the brothy rice noodles out of the soup spoon hovering on top of my big bowl of beef pho. Slurping seems to be the only way to really enjoy this Vietnamese noodle soup, but no one is doing so among the largely Asian crowd in the small restaurant.

Will is not with us today so Leon and I are sharing a small corner table. I look up as he says, "What about this Sunday for that dinner you agreed to have with me?"

The very question I've been waiting for. By asking Laure for the favor of giving me a day off, Leon has made sure my answer would be yes. But, at that instant, I get it in my head to tease him, do the measly bit I could so things aren't a little too easy for him. Just as it bugged me once that he had me followed to find out where I lived, it annoys me that he can ask—maybe, expect—Laure to give me a Sunday off. Except when there's a good reason, like the overused crisis or death-in-the-family sob story, few of us cooks and chefs would think of asking Laure for time off on weekends, the busiest nights at Du Cœur. Especially when it's only for a date, and on such short notice.

I scowl and put on what I hope is a disappointed pout. "I can't. How can you ask me to go out on a Sunday? You know I'm working, and that happens to be a very busy night."

Leon's jaw drops for an instant. "What? I don't understand. Didn't Laure tell you?"

I deepen my scowl. "Tell me what?"

He shakes his head. "She couldn't have forgotten. That's so unlike her."

"You still haven't said what she's supposed to have told me."

Leon stares at me for some moments without saying anything. He frowns, turns his head sideways, and regards me from the sides of his eyes. "She did tell you, I'm sure of it. She's giving you Sunday off, isn't she?"

"Why would she do that?" I am actually getting tired of this silly, spur-of-the-moment game I started, because I haven't a clue how to end it.

"Because I asked her. Damn it. She's always gone along with what I've asked of her."

Leon is losing his cool—I didn't foresee this. I'm not quite sure how else to react beyond my startled reaction to his outburst.

He apologizes immediately after, so I say nothing.

There's still a fierceness in his eyes and I avert mine to concentrate on the fragrant bowl of soup in front of me. I inhale its vapors, trying to guess what spices and herbs may be in it. I can always find any recipe on the internet, but I get a kick out of guessing the ingredients in a dish and learning later that my guesses are right. I inhale once again. Star anise, for sure. My mother likes to use it. When I was a child, she laid a piece of the chocolate brown star-shaped spice in the palm of my hand. I thought it quite pretty. But when she held it next to my nose to smell, I was hooked. It has a fragrance I've never forgotten.

I sneak a glance at Leon. He's turned his attention back to his bigger bowl of pho. He also seems absorbed, his gaze fixed on his soup as he picks up a piece of beef. But his mind is elsewhere.

It's time to make amends. I say, "This is good, isn't it? Maybe Will would have liked it, too."

"He does, but I sent him on an errand. Anyway, he won't be coming with us any longer."

It may have been odd that Will came with us in the first place; as his employer, Leon can always tell him what to do. But it seems unfair that, once again, Leon can so easily get his way. Maybe it's unreasonable for me to expect it but I would have liked to have been asked, since the three of us were having fun together. Still, all I say is "I like Will. I liked having him around."

"You'll still see him. If you want and if it makes you feel safer, I can ask him to drive us to dinner on Sunday." Leon is watching me, his lips twitching into an amused smile. "I'd rather not, of course."

He does have an irresistible smile and my silly game has exhausted its appeal to me. So I return his smile. "I'm sorry Leon. Laure did give me the night off. Do you still want to go out with me?"

"What do you think?"

*****

The restaurant we go to is three times the size of Du Cœur, a big institutional-style dining hall with a high ceiling, concrete flooring, and long communal tables and benches, at the end of which is a big open kitchen. In the middle of the kitchen, an open brick-walled grill is ablaze, small vaporous orange flames shooting up from its wide expanse. Several cooks are tending the grill and it's clear this is where much of the cooking is taking place.

The layout of the restaurant seems guaranteed to amplify sounds—surely not a place for intimate conversations. People are flanked by strangers and everyone seems to be talking all at once. I feel like I'm in a bustling market where customers haggle over every purchase they make.

But I get into the spirit of the place. It's hard not to when it's buzzing with laughter and excited voices. And I understand that excitement when I taste the dishes I order. I do believe in the power of tasty well-prepared food to put people in a pleasant, sociable mood. It doesn't take fancy dishes like those we offer at Du Cœur. Those dishes are delicious, beautiful, and innovative all at the same time. They demand your attention. At this restaurant, the food is like a backdrop. It's not what you focus on. It's there to enjoy but also to put you in the mood for a good time with friends.

Ingredients are fresh and—you could say—upscale, but they're familiar to most diners. My main course has wild mushrooms cooked by the fire, topped by a perfectly cooked egg. It's a type of restaurant I wouldn't mind owning in the future.

I smile happily at Leon, who's sitting to my right and at the end of the dark rough-hewn trestle table. He gives me back a bright smile, and I wonder for a moment why he would choose to dine here since this evening is supposed to be our first time to be alone together.

Apart from comments about food and bits of gossip about goings-on at the restaurant, Leon and I don't talk much. This would have been the time for us to get to know each other better, but in choosing this admittedly delightful but noisy place, Leon has made it impossible to do so.

We leave the restaurant less than two hours later, with bellies full, and smiles still on our faces. At Du Cœur, most clients stay over three hours.

Leon drives me straight home to my apartment. He stops his car in front of it and says, "I hope you had a good time. I'll see you tomorrow for lunch?"

"Yes, I had a good time. Thank you so much." I'm a little bewildered as I'm saying this. I guess I imagined a different kind of evening.

Leon gets out of the car and goes around it to open my door for me. As I step out onto the curb, I say,

"Would you like to come up for a minute? Maybe you'd like to see how the lower ten percent of us live?"

He laughs. I was teasing and I'm glad he takes it graciously.

Chapter Eighteen

After Dinner

My apartment is not a home I'd be proud of and, surely, not one I'd show off. Except for my family on their rare visits, and Brent when he picked me up for dinner at Marcia's, no one else has been in it. Anyway, I would not invite anyone into it by choice, unless I can't help it. But this evening, I wanted Leon to see it.

Maybe, I do want to open his eyes to how we live, those of us who aren't born with silver spoons in our mouths. Those who have to struggle for things that Leon can get, by merely opening his mouth or flicking his finger. Or, maybe, I'm testing him. I want him to see how different our worlds are; how far apart we are from each other. When he sees my world, will he still love me? Really love me? The Me inside the pretty shell he sees. That Me who lives within the narrow confines of bare, ugly walls when she's not working as a kitchen grunt.

Somehow I know Brent wouldn't care. But Leon?

Inside the apartment, Leon stands undecided, his gaze quickly sweeping across the small room that holds my bed, a nondescript dining table with four chairs, and an ample armchair next to my bed.

"Please take a seat," I say, amused to see him hesitate. "The armchair is very comfortable. I may get another one like it when I have enough money saved up,"

"Thank you," he says, sitting down.

"Would you like anything to drink? I can make us some coffee."

"No, no. Please don't bother. Let's just talk. We never had much chance for anything but trivia at the restaurant."

I sit down on the bed across from Leon. "Nice place for dinner even so. Great food, happy people all around you—can't help but be happy yourself."

"Yes, I felt the same way." He lifts the armchair off the worn-out rug to turn and face me.

"Have you been there before?"

Leon shakes his head. ""No. One of my employees suggested it."

"That means you took your former girlfriends to fancy places."

He scowls but his lips break slowly into a smile of amusement. "Well, yes. Most of them haven't been to a place like Du Cœur so they're eager to go. You're the first one who wanted something like the restaurant we went to tonight."

"Did you mind?"

"No. I was pleasantly surprised. The chef is good and he has something there that appeals to people. I did know it gets noisy. My employee warned me. Anyway, it's too early for us to hold hands at dinner so that restaurant is perfect for a first date."

I laugh and say, "Are you planning every stage of ... our courtship? I guess that's what it is. Sounds so old-fashioned, though—courtship. Nowadays, it seems people hop into bed after they've just met."

Leon chuckles. "Looks like I'm planning it, but only in my head. You could say I'm doing what I can to ensure success."

"I see. But you know I'm on to you. Your so-called 'love' for me will only last as long as you're having fun. Or until someone else comes along who entices you more. Marcia warned me."

"But Marcia doesn't know how I really feel about you."

I shrug. "Maybe not. But you must admit your track record for being faithful isn't good. Maybe she's right that it's the pursuit you enjoy most."

"Not true, although wooing an attractive woman does energize me. Anyway, you're different."

"How can you be so sure? I'm as ordinary as they come. Besides, how much do you really know about me?"

Leon smiles. "More than you might think."

"Why? Did you have some investigator pry into my life? I know you had me followed, maybe by Will, to find out where I live."

His smile turns into an embarrassed grimace. "I admit I did that. I couldn't get you out of my mind. And Laure wouldn't give me your phone number. I had to let you know how I felt."

"Well, now I do know."

"Then, can I hope that you'll return my feelings?"

I sigh. "You are getting to me. But who knows what'll happen. Anyway, I can't allow myself to fall deeply in love with you because you'll tire of me sometime."

Leon winces. "That makes me sound ... like an asshole."

"Well, you are, in some ways. But you're also smart, sweet, thoughtful, very much the gentleman, and quite attractive. Anyway, we grew up worlds apart, and I'm curious what it's like—your world. Marcia says, I should take what you offer, just have fun while all this lasts. I've taken her advice. There, I've laid both our cards on the table."

Leon stares at me, saying nothing. I stare back, waiting for him to speak.

Finally, he says, "I did tell you once that you're rather direct. It's good. I like it. But I don't like the sound of the cards you've laid on the table."

"You know what? Neither do I. You say it makes you sound like an asshole. I come out as an opportunist. But I'm only saying what any relationship with you would be like. You've got a history. I'm a blank slate. The one year Adam and I were together is nothing. What does a nineteen-year old really know of serious relationships?"

"What if our relationship deepens?"

"Then I guess we could have a happy-ever-after. But I'm sure that's a long shot. Anyway, you should be glad I'm going into this with my eyes open. I won't do a Cristi on you."

"What if I ask you to marry me?"

I can't help laughing. "You can't be serious."

Leon regards me intently. He reaches over, takes my left hand, and encloses it in both of his. "I am, actually. You've affected me in a way no other woman has. I can see myself spending the best years of my life with you. I won't pledge my whole life. Who knows what the future will bring? As it is, at least fifty percent of marriages end in divorce. How can anyone believe in everlasting love?"

"Yeah, how can anyone? But my parents have been together for ages. Is that everlasting love? Anyway, I think you're still here because you haven't won me yet."

"You really don't think too highly of me, do you? Or are you just distrustful of people, in general?"

It's my turn to be silent. Once again, I don't know what to say to Leon. Can I believe him? It's a heady, incredible thought—that I could be married to this filthy-rich, good-looking guy. So what if it only lasts a few years? We may not have the kind of soulful love I could have had with Brent but I might have the best time of my life. Did I just say that—a soulful love? I have to think about that later because I'm not sure what it means.

But I can't believe Leon just yet. "Maybe, I'm distrustful, by nature. You said years. But can you stand one woman that long? From what Marcia says, you go through a new one about every three or four months. Cristi only lasted two."

"That's because I met you."

"No. It's because she was spooking you out. Anyway, odds are you'll meet someone who fascinates you more, let's say, in a month."

Leon shakes his head. "I've met many women since I met you. How long ago was that? Four, five months? I'm still here."

"True enough. But maybe for you, success means luring a woman to your bed. After the first time, she becomes less and less exciting; until two or three months later, you tell her it's all over."

"That was before I met you."

"Right. I bet you say that to all the girls."

"No. Honestly. You're the first. Why don't you try me? Live with me; let's see where it goes. After all, you said you're willing to be in a relationship with me just for fun. See what it's like to be rich."

"Oh Leon, be serious. You've never done anything like this."

"I never wanted to live with anyone before. But I want to try, with you."

"But I'm not sure I love you."

"Don't you? Just a little?"

"You're quite attractive, I've said so."

"That's a good start. Can you imagine us making love?"

I'm not a virgin, but Leon's question makes me blush. Is it from embarrassment? Or is it excitement? "Yes," I say truthfully. I can feel my cheeks burning.

Leon leans over to kiss my lips. I let him but I don't return his kiss. He peers into my face, straightens up, and leans back on the chair.

I say, "I'm sorry, Leon. I'm not ready for this."

"I won't rush you. But can you promise to think about what I'm proposing? Let's live together; see where that leads us. Who knows, maybe we'll find out we can't live without each other."

"Or we can't stand each other. And what if only one of us realizes he can't live without the other?"

Leon shrugs. "I guess that's a risk we take." He glances at his watch and gets up from the chair. "I have to go. It's late. I have work tomorrow."

*****

Just before midnight, I dial Brent's number. I feel as if I need to hear his reassuring voice.

He answers right away. "Regine, this is a most wonderful surprise."

"I'm sorry to be calling so late. I hope this isn't a bad time."

"No, it's quite all right. I don't often go to bed before 1 AM. Besides, I once bothered you at midnight. So we're even. What can I do for you? You and I have been out of touch for a while."

"I just wanted someone to talk to and you're the only one I know who's still up at this time." Why can't I be as direct with Brent as I am with Leon? It is him and no one else who I want to talk to tonight.

"I see. Well, I'm all ears."

"How have you been? Have you seen Marcia lately?"

"No, but I'm having dinner at her place next Monday. You must know that she invited me. I can't resist another great dinner."

"Yes, she told me. I hope you two have fun together."

"I'll try my best. How about you? Been seeing Leon lately?"

"Yes. We've been exploring small quirky places for lunch. With his driver Will. And actually Leon just left here half an hour ago. We had dinner at a restaurant he's never tried before."

"Was Will with you?" I hear amusement in his voice.

I chuckle. "No, of course not."

"It sounds like you're getting serious."

"He asked me to live with him."

There, I've blurted it out. Tell me what I should do, Brent. Tell me you don't want me to. Tell me you love me.

He's silent for a few moments. I hold my breath, dreading what he might say.

"Did you say yes?"

"No."

"Would you like to say yes?"

"I'm tempted," I say, feeling defeated. Tell me you don't want me to.

Silence, again. "Good luck, then, child, whatever you decide to do."

"I'm not a child," I say, on reflex. I'm sure that did make me sound like a petulant child, but he's infuriated me. Why can't he see? But why can't I tell him how I feel?

"No, you're not a child. I'm sorry if I offended you. I didn't mean to. But I'm tired, and I'm afraid I have to say good night."

"Good night." But I can't put the phone down and Brent doesn't hang up.

Seconds later, he says, "I'll be thinking of you. Always."

I hang up and burst into tears. Why couldn't I tell him how I feel?

A week later and I still haven't said yes to Leon's proposal. He doesn't press me for an answer, and we continue our little adventures of holes-in-the-wall lunches. Before we part one Tuesday, he takes me in his arms and kisses me.

The lingering taste of our lunch is still on his lips and I kiss him back. I pull away, but not before I kiss him on both cheeks. Then, I open the car door and run up to my apartment.

*****

When I arrive at the restaurant on Wednesday the following week, Marcia catches my eye and inclines her head towards the door. Anxious to start my work, I shake my head. She approaches me and grabbing my elbow, she leads me out of the kitchen.

She says, "Five minutes. Maybe ten. Laure won't mind."

Her eyes are glowing and I detect a blush on her cheeks. I smile, amused at her excitement. "What's up?"

"Brent spent the night at my apartment," she says, returning my smile, baring her straight white teeth.

I suppress an involuntary gulp of air into my gut, struggle to keep my mouth stretched into a smile, but my insides have turned sour. What does one say to unwelcome news from a friend, my best friend?

"Don't you want to know how it went?"

"Tell me," I say, looking away. I guess I'm fortunate Marcia is too excited to notice the quiver in my voice.

"Well, first we had dinner, of course. Brent loved my porchetta, which I made using my mother's recipe. I can give ..." I can barely listen as I swallow acid coming up from my gut. ... "We also had the most luscious strawberries for dessert."

"Sounds delicious." It's all I can think of to say.

"Yeah. Everything was like a dream. Passion is a word invented for Brent."

"So, you got him to 'roll in the hay'." I try to sound light-hearted.

"And how!" Marcia is floating on cloud nine. I don't think she'd notice if tears were to start rolling down my cheeks.

"You must have changed your mind, then, about whether he's your happily-ever-after."

"Not just yet. I want to test him a little longer. I welcome his intense side in my bed. But over the dinner table? I'll have to see. I tried last night to keep him from talking about his work."

Not until I'm soaking in the tub do I think again about my conversation with Marcia. A conversation that, without her knowing, has decided my fate.

I tell myself I can't be jealous of Marcia. She's my best friend. And Brent, it seems, has chosen her. At that thought, tears begin to well up and blur my vision. Tears I can't control until they drop into the bubbly water and disappear. Quiet tears that keep going. Now I know why I couldn't tell Brent how I felt. I was afraid he couldn't return my feelings. Afraid of the pain that was sure to follow. The pain that now has me in its grip.

I lean back against the tub, rest my head, and close my eyes. About half an hour later, I jerk myself upright, shivering in water that has turned cold. I must have fallen asleep.

The next day, I greet Marcia with my brightest smile.

Spur-of-the Moment Decision

Move on. That's become my mantra since the first time I remember saying it to myself, when I said no to Adam's proposal of marriage. The choice had been mine from the start, though made on the fly. No one and nothing forced it on me. It's a clear decision I've never regretted. One that opened up a new world to me. A challenging, exciting world.

But life has grown murkier since. The second time I uttered that mantra was after the stabbing incident and its long, drawn-out consequences. I've moved on, but the shadow of that incident remains in my guilt for whatever part I played in Cristi's misery. Her accusations were unfounded—I know that in my brain—but guilt, I think, gets planted more deeply in our guts, our hearts. It endures like embers that keep giving off heat even when you can no longer see them glow.

This time, the third in just over three years, I say it to myself again. Move on. This time, though, I do so with a heavy heart. I tell myself that Brent was never mine to give up. We had that short period when I was sure there was something deep that bound us to each other. But it seems, that was merely my illusion.

The days that follow Marcia's recounting of her night with Brent are, for me, a trial. I guess her happiness needs to be talked about again and again. I listen, often with a forced, fixed smile, and say very little as she discloses, bit by bit, their passionate night together. All I can do is swallow more than my usual number of antacid pills afterward.

Marcia and Brent are having another dinner at her condo in two weeks. I'm dreading the days that will come after that. Marcia will have more stories, but they'll be variations on those she's told me already.

*****

Hours before the night of their dinner, I take some decisive steps.

Leon has never come back up to my apartment since that first time, and he's waiting in his car. Earlier, he called me to say we're going to a new mom-and-pop Caribbean place people are raving about on Twitter.

As I plop my butt down into the passenger seat of Leon's car, I touch his knee. The gesture is intimate and unexpected. It startles him. I'm aware I've been more cool and casual with him than I actually feel. I've grown to like him a lot, but in a way different from how I feel about Brent.

I say, "I'm feeling reckless today. I just realized I've never been to your house. Do you have time to show it to me? I can make us something quick and simple for lunch. I'm good at cobbling a meal together from what you have in your refrigerator."

Leon's face lights up. "Caribbean food can wait and my work can wait. Having you cook for me is too tempting to pass up. I have a pad on Claremont Hills, a mere ten minutes from here."

The "pad" Leon takes me to is four times as large as my parents' home, and when I lived there, the modest house handled the chaos created by six people. I see no one about when we get to Leon's house, but he says he lives in it with a housekeeper, a cook, and Will, although Will only stays a few nights a week. He has a family in Vacaville, thirty miles inland.

This is my first glimpse into a house of the rich and it's nothing like what I imagined from television. For one, it's not full of the kind of furniture you find in European castles and palaces. My first impression is of one large living space.

We pass an area furnished with oversized, very modern furniture. Farther in are a kitchen and dining area. No walls separate these areas. Seeing this house, I fully understand Leon's reaction when he came up to my apartment. To him, my apartment must have seemed like the pits. Worse than a doghouse.

"Wow! This is where you live?" I say.

He laughs. "If you think this is huge, you have to see my parents' house, our family home in the Los Altos hills. Much larger."

"How can your housekeeper keep up this place?"

"She gets cleaners to come and do the job. I'm not quite sure how she manages this house. I just pay her to do whatever is needed. Come on and see what's in the refrigerator."

As I'm foraging in the vegetable and meat compartments, a middle-aged man comes in and I hear Leon say, "I don't need you to make me anything, Luciano. I brought a chef from a high-class restaurant to do that for me today. So, just go back to whatever you're doing. We'll need someone to clean up later, though. Can you tell Sara please?"

I straighten up, a carton of eggs and a bag of chanterelles in my hands. I see Luciano walking out a backdoor. "Is Luciano your cook?"

"Yes, he cooked for an upscale Italian restaurant, but he burned out before he was fifty. I offered him this job, with generous perks and hardly any stress. He's good but his dishes are a little more traditional and, of course, his bias is for Italian cooking. He will experiment, though, and he has an instinct for flavors that go well together."

"Does he mind that I'm invading his kitchen?"

"I don't know. You're the first chef I've ever brought home."

I show Leon what I intend to make. "I'll do a take on the dinner we had. This is the quickest dish I can cook."

I place the eggs and mushrooms on the counter and I take out an onion and a carton of crème fraîche.

"A splash of white wine would be good with the mushrooms. Chardonnay, maybe."

Leon opens a drawer that holds bottles of wine. He shows me a chardonnay. "I think this should do."

It took me twenty minutes to slice the onion and chanterelles, and sauté them with some wine, thyme, and tarragon. Just before I take the pan off the burner, I swirl in a dollop of crème fraiche. I top the sautéed mushrooms with the eggs, which were frying in another pan.

We sit down at a breakfast table in the middle of the kitchen and devour our quick lunch with a baguette.

"Delicious," Leon says, spearing mushrooms into his mouth. "I have to tell Luciano about this."

"Well, it helped that you have all these ingredients lying around."

"That's Luciano. He keeps the refrigerator well stocked. Every morning, he goes out to a bakery by the hotel for his fix of croissants. He usually brings home a baguette and some other artisan bread."

When we finish eating, Leon reaches over to my hand, which is resting on the table, and squeezes it. "Does this mean yes? You'll come live with me?"

I stare straight into his eyes, searching. I don't know what I'm looking for or what I expect to find— some indication that he's sincere about asking me to live with him, or that he really loves me?

He stares back at me with an earnestness that makes me smile. In a moment of daring, I say, "Not quite yet. Make love to me, then I'll tell you for sure."

Those words came out of me as if on impulse, but if some therapist were to tell me that Marcia's recent escapades with Brent were behind that impulse, I wouldn't argue against it.

I can't take those words back. I won't, anyway, even if I could. I've wondered what it's like making love with Leon, and I'm about to find out. At our next break, I'll have something I can tell Marcia. Next time, she'll have to listen to me.

My hand on his knee caused Leon to raise his brow and grin. This time, I watch, wickedly amused, when his jaw drops and his brow rises even higher. But he's dumbfounded for only a few seconds. He rises from his chair, pulls me up from mine, and gathers me in his arms. He kisses me—long and deep kisses that leave me breathless. I taste the chanterelles in his mouth, sniff the chardonnay on his breath, and kiss him back just as fiercely. Raising my arms, I entwine them around his neck and press my body to his. The last time I had sex was three years ago, and I must be hungry for this melding of bodies. Leon scoops me up in his arms and carries me up to his bedroom.

As he carries me up the stairs and down the hallway, I feel inexplicably shy and nervous. If I now have misgivings about going on with what I've started, it's too late. I close my eyes and bury my face against Leon's neck. I open my eyes only when he's laying me down on the bed.

He takes off my clothes and I rub my legs and arms on the sheets. They caress my skin, their silkiness so like the cool, smooth skin of a ripe nectarine. I sink a little deeper into the pillow-soft mattress as it cradles my body in soothing warmth. I imagine myself crawling into this luxurious bed every night and waking up in it every morning. I could get used to this way too easily.

Leon's face hovers over mine and we lock eyes for an instant before his lips claim mine again. He kisses me all over my face and my neck, and his lips wander all over my body, nibbling and tasting, lingering on my nipples.

I can feel his bare skin against mine, and his hands roaming all over my body. I close my eyes again as he thrusts into me.

Although I haven't quite forgotten what it's like to make love, I lie passive, hesitant. Leon stops and says, "Am I hurting you?"

I shake my head. "It's been a while."

"Do you want me to stop?"

I shake my head again. He resumes thrusting, a little more slowly. Leon is responsive and gentle—I like that about him. All the experience he has with women seems to have taught him well.

It doesn't take long before I cling to him and answer his every thrust. As we climb the peak of feverish passion, Leon seems to get lost in it, and he's no longer there with me. I leave him and go after my own pleasure; but when it comes, it's Brent's name that I nearly shout out.

I meant to let go of any hopes that Brent might love me, so it's a shock that he snatches my most intense moment of lovemaking from Leon. When Leon, exhausted and satiated, lays his head against my shoulder, I wrap my arms around him, trying to atone for what would have been an unforgivable slip.

Minutes later, Leon murmurs, "Do you love me just a little?

I nod and kiss the top of his head. But I wonder. Am I lying to both of us?

I believe Leon's rich parents brought him up to be self-centered. It shows in his assurance that he can get anything he wants. I also sense it in the way he gets so consumed by his passion that you feel you're just a vessel for it. But maybe everyone is like that. He can be patient, though, just before those moments. And that makes him a good lover. Besides, I can't deny that he has seduced me with his charms. And his lifestyle. Do I love him? I think so; at least a little.

Leon is no saint, but neither am I. I know he can't commit to one woman, but I am in this relationship—as he is well aware of—partly because he's opening doors into a world I've only seen in my imagination or in the fantasy world of movies and television. Maybe we do suit each other. Maybe Brent belongs to a higher sphere, a noble one we can't aspire to.

On this afternoon, Leon doesn't return to work and I don't go back to my apartment. The following morning, he drives me straight to Du Cœur.

He wants me to move in with him right away. Now that we've had our first night together, he tells me he can't live without me. Maybe he means what he says but I have to keep reminding myself that "faithful" is a concept alien to Leon.

"But Leon," I say. "I need to pack and I won't have time to do it until Monday."

"Bring a suitcase of clothes and we can get the rest later." He winks at me, "Or I can buy you a new wardrobe."

"Just like that? I'm not sure I can do this. I've never lived with anyone."

"Neither have I. Think of it as an experiment. Or an exotic new dish you're trying out. Aren't you eager to know if it'll work out?" He grins and winks at me again. "Anyway, now you'll experience how the rich live."

I return his grin. "Well, if you put it that way. I guess it'll be like taking a vacation from my doghouse ..."

Leon frowns, "Your doghouse? You have no dog."

"A private joke. Nothing more. Anyway, I should tell my mother we're doing this."

Leon laughs, pauses, and regards me with a raised eyebrow. "You're not kidding, are you?"

"No. I'm not asking for her permission, but this is a big change and I have to let my family know."

He takes me in his arms and plants a kiss on my forehead. "Of course. I do understand. Do whatever you need to do. I'm sure I can survive without you for a week or two. Or can I?"

How long this fairy tale will last, I can't tell. And by history—Leon's history, that is—this fairy tale won't have a happy ending. I tell myself I'm fully aware of what I'm getting into. But will that be enough to prepare me for the day when Leon says our relationship is no longer where he wants to be?

The next time I talk to Marcia, I tell her as casually as I can that I'm moving in with Leon. As I expected, she asks me about the night I spent with him. But I realize then that some things are just too private to share with anyone else but the person you have the experience with, so I can't get myself to be as open as Marcia is about them. More so because, frankly, I don't want her blabbing to Brent about what I say it's like making love with Leon. If he really wants to know, which I doubt, Brent can call and ask me. So I answer Marcia's question with a shrug and say that nothing can be as passionate as what she has with Brent.

The Experiment

You"ve broken a record," Marcia says.

"What record, exactly?'

"Why kiddo—endurance! How long has it been since that first note from Leon? Seven, eight months? Now you're even living together."

I shrug. "Maybe, he's getting tired of playing around."

She nods thoughtfully. "Conceivable. Is he getting restless yet?"

"Doesn't seem like it."

"Now, that is remarkable. And you've been living together two months."

"I think it's my cooking."

"Naah. He can hire the best cook on the planet."

"I was kidding. I think Leon is just older, more mature."

"No, it's more than that. You've somehow seduced him."

"How did I do that? I asked him to turn his attention to someone else. But he persisted."

"Maybe, that's it. Playing hard to get."

"I wasn't playing. I was just being me. No scheming. No going out of my way to seduce him. Not even now."

"You must entice him in some way—that's why he's still with you."

"Yeah, with a witch's brew I make him drink every night." Marcia is beginning to annoy me.

She laughs. "I'm sorry. You're right. There's no point to this conversation. Maybe, next week, you'll break up." She pauses, winks at me. "Or Leon might ask you to marry him."

Marcia believes breaking up with Leon is imminent. A matter of time. She's right, of course. The truth is, I am afraid of hoping, of being drawn deeper into a relationship with Leon. In little ways, I've tried to preserve some semblance of separateness. It's not hard to do, since we have different working hours, and often he's asleep when I come home from the restaurant. Marcia is right about another thing: It's remarkable Leon hasn't yet shown signs of restlessness.

I haven't heard from Brent since that night I called him. I expect I'll never see him again. Marcia has stopped talking about their passionate trysts after I refused to disclose details of my nights with Leon.

Marcia and Brent continue to see each other, although she's more convinced now that Brent is a fling, a long one that will end when one of them decides it has run its course.

*****

"What is it like, living with the rich?" Mom says in her most recent phone call. Mom's Tuesday night phone calls have become part of my routine. They usually come around six in the evening, before Leon comes home from work. I recline in comfort on the couch, ready for a call that can last as long as a half hour. Tonight, I wonder why she has waited this long to ask me this question.

"To be frank, aside from the large fancy house, not having to clean up, having breakfasts brought to our room every morning, and trips when Leon can take off on Mondays and Tuesdays, nothing much has really changed. I'm working just as hard and Leon is often asleep by the time I get home."

Mom laughs. "You think that's nothing much? What I'd give just to have breakfasts in bed and have someone else clean up the mess in the house. Occasional trips and a beautiful house with lots of space are like hitting the jackpot twice. But you're discovering the drudgery of living together and that's good. It's a test of how much and how long you can stand each other."

"I guess you're right. We're still together, despite the daily grind, and that must say a lot. Especially with Leon. We do have lots of fun on our little trips. I've seen more of California in the last two months than I've ever had in my whole life before Leon. I had my first plane ride and it was in his family's plane."

"Have you met his family?" Mom sounds incredulous.

"No. It was just Leon and me and a plane crew. He knows how to fly a plane but he says his father won't allow anyone in his family to fly it."

"Do you know his family?"

"Leon doesn't like talking about them, which is just as well. Mom, you know I'm not expecting this thing to last. I'm just having fun."

"I know you said so. But I can't help it if it makes me sad to see you hold no hope for a future together."

Mom's remark gives me pause. "Mom, please don't worry about me. I'm stronger than Cristi."

"I know you are; but is it really worth it?"

"I don't know, Mom. I often ask myself the same question. The thing is, right now, I really am enjoying myself and I find that hard to give up."

"Then I guess I should shut up. It's just that I was brought up to believe everything we do has a purpose."

"Can't enjoying myself count as a purpose?"

"I do want you to be happy, and since you sound happy, then I should be satisfied. But ..."

"But what?"

"I know you're not fragile like Cristi, but what if you fall deeply in love with Leon?"

Again, she gives me pause. "I don't know, Mom. I guess I'll be heartbroken."

"That's what I'm afraid of."

"Well, there's a first time for everything," I say, trying to make light of her apprehension. "I'll take it as a good learning experience."

"I'm not so sure it'll be easy to say that when you're really hurting."

When she hangs up, I don't spring up from the couch to see what Luciano is preparing for dinner. I stay, mulling over our conversation. Why have I never thought of my relationship with Leon as just a fling, like Marcia says hers is with Brent?

The answer—when it comes to me—is unsettling. Whether I wanted to or not, I am emotionally involved. My relationship with Leon is not just a fling, a fact that opens me up to being hurt. And the longer I stay, the deeper I am involved. The deeper the hurt. Maybe I should leave, end this "experiment," throw out this new "dish" before I sink too deeply to get out of it relatively unscathed.

I hear the garage door open. Leon is home. Must put off making a decision.

But a couple of weeks pass without me thinking of the matter again. It's easy to get so caught up in all the things I need to do every day that I never find time to think.

One evening at dinner, Leon says, "I haven't met your parents. How about we go pay them a visit?"

Amazed and bewildered, I stare at Leon. Then, this thought comes to me: A visit will reassure Mom. So, a visit is good. But will it also give her false hopes?

Leon sees me hesitate. "What's the matter? Don't you want me to meet them?"

"Why do you want to meet my family? I know you're not so eager for me to meet yours, but that's okay. We know what we have will end, maybe next month, next week. But that's also a good reason not to meet mine."

Leon puts his fork down. "Let me make this quite clear first: I have no intention of breaking up. Not next week. Not even next month. I hope you don't, either. You've talked about your mother. I think she's someone I'd like to meet. Besides, I'm curious what made you so lovable."

"Yeah, right," I say. But I blush—his compliment is not lost on me. I'm as much a sucker as any other female for a man's white lies. "Can I at least give them warning that we intend to visit?"

*****

Two weeks later, Leon and I visit my parents on a Saturday afternoon. I asked Laure for a few hours off, but not before I told Leon I didn't want him asking Laure for any special favors on my behalf. I don't want to abuse her good will. I will be at work at eight when the restaurant is at its busiest.

My whole family is waiting for us when we arrive. Mom opens the door and behind her stands my father. After I introduce Leon to my parents, they lead us into the living room. The television—usually on even when no one is watching—has been turned off.

Mom must have told everyone to be on good behavior. My two youngest brothers are on the floor putting away pieces of a construction set. Sabine and Maurice are reading books, rare for Maurice.

Dad introduces my sister and brothers to Leon, pointing to each one. They briefly smile, wave once, and say nothing. If Mom told them earlier Leon is quite rich, not one is showing signs of being impressed.

When it's Bernie's turn, he approaches Leon and shakes his hand. "How do you do, Mr. Leon Barrett."

Leon grins. "Very well, Mr. Bernie Lambert. How do you do?"

"Welcome to our humble abode. Mom made some treats, so you must be pretty special. She only makes them on birthdays and holidays. I think she cooks better than Gina so I'm sure you'll love them."

Everyone laughs and with that, we all begin to relax.

Mom says, "Since Bernie already gave our surprise away, why don't we talk around the dining table. I have soda, tea, coffee, and, of course, bottled sparkling water."

I raise an eyebrow at my mother. The family gets bottled water only on Mom's rare trips to a big outlet store, and like canned soda, she doles it out sparingly.

On the dining table are three covered platters. As she takes the covers off of each, Mom says to Leon, "What will you have Leon? Coffee, tea, soda?"

"Coffee, please."

"Coffee for grown-ups, then," she says as she goes into the kitchen. "Come, Sabine, I need your help."

On the three platters are some family favorites that Mom usually makes on holidays and birthdays: gougères, almond cream fig tart, and salted caramelized walnuts.

Grinning, Leon says to Bernie, "You're right, looks like we're in for some seriously delicious treats."

Bernie grins and gives a thumbs-up. "Yeah, thanks to you." He points to the gougères. "These are my favorite. Cheesy cream puffs. But they're all good."

Gerard says, "Me, I like the fruit tart. It's got almond cream in it. Mom always makes it on Thanksgiving. But you have to like figs."

Leon says, "I like figs."

Gerard says, "Me, too. We have a fig tree in the back yard."

Sabine returns with utensils, six cups and saucers, and two cans of soda on a tray. She gives the soda to Gerard and Bernie. "Wait to be served, okay? Mom will be here in a minute."

Dad sits at the head of the table, watching everyone. He smiles, but has said nothing since he made the introductions. Although he's never much of a talker, I feel a little uncomfortable about his silence today, so I say, "How's work, Dad?

He shrugs his shoulders. "Nothing new. The usual."

I nod, regretting that I said anything at all to him. I've never known what to say to my father to induce him to reveal his intimate thoughts. None of us children are particularly close to him, although he and the boys often watch ball games together.

I remember, growing up, that he always came home exhausted from work. The first thing he does when he arrives is take a shower while Mom makes dinner with help from Sabine, and from me when I still lived at home. Then, he plants himself in front of the television and doesn't budge until someone calls him for dinner. He always eats voraciously and quickly. As he finishes his bottle of beer, he watches us eat and when his bottle is finished, he says, "So, how did everybody's day go today?"

We all say "Okay" simultaneously and once in a while, Bernie—after he started going to school—has a little news to share. I suspect Dad is not that interested in his or our news; in asking about our day, he's calling our attention to his presence. It's his way of declaring that we—him, in particular—are all there, at home at the end of the day.

As far as I know, Cristi's father, Raf, is his only friend in the neighborhood. They occasionally go somewhere to do things together. He might have some friends at work, but we've never met them and he hardly talks about them.

Dad looks uncomfortable with Leon, and Leon doesn't seem to know what to say to him. Were it not for the two youngest boys, any conversation that takes place while Mom and Sabine are in the kitchen would have to be between Leon and me.

Mom returns shortly, carrying a tray with a pot of coffee, a carafe of milk and a bowl of sugar. She serves

Leon first, tells him to help himself to whatever he wants.

Leon says, "Thank you. They all look scrumptious." He takes a piece from each platter.

Mom serves my father next, gives him a cup of coffee and a plateful of everything. She hands me, Sabine, and Maurice cups of coffee and plates.

I take a couple of gougères.

While taking another gougère, Leon says, "These are truly special. I see where Gina gets her talent."

Bernie butts in with a broad, triumphant smile. "I told you, didn't I?"

Leon nods at him and turns to my mother again. "May I ask how you learned to make them?"

For a few moments, Mom says nothing and looks away. This isn't the first time someone has asked her this question, which always brings back painful memories of her father. When finally she speaks, there's a break in her voice too obvious for Leon to miss. "My father was a French chef."

Leon's face is a picture of obvious admiration, mixed with incredulity. Mom's response leaves him with nothing to say.

My family knows Mom is struggling with her emotions, so we say nothing and let her be until she regains composure. Once in a while, she leaves us to sit in the bedroom alone for a while. But with Leon among us, the silence feels awkward to me. And Mom's gaze is still directed away from all of us, as if she's forgotten that we are there.

I break the silence, asking Maurice and Sabine which of Mom's snacks they like best. Food and eating are always safe topics. I watch Mom as Leon chimes in with his own remarks about Maurice's and Sabine's choices. Before long, Mom looks at me and smiles.

She turns to Leon and asks if he has any brothers and sisters. I watch Leon, curious about what he will say. I once asked him about his family. He scowled in irritation and said he would prefer not to talk about them. I never brought that subject up again.

It takes him a moment to answer, but when he does, he's his usual polished and charming self. He says, "I have a brother, the youngest in the family. He's away at school. My sister is married and lives out of state."

Mom nods but seems at a loss, with nothing else to say. I doubt she has any real interest in Leon's brother and sister beyond what Leon has already told her. Either out of politeness or a desire to avoid any more questions about his family, Leon says, "Mrs. Lambert, can you share your recipes? If you don't mind, I'd like to pass them on to my cook."

At the mention of a cook, Bernie perks up. "You have a cook? Wow! Cool."

Mom says, "No, I don't mind. I'll write them out and send them to Gina."

Our visit ends after another quarter hour talking about food and Bernie's adventures in school.

On the way to Du Cœur, I wonder if Leon would be curious enough to ask me what upset my mother when he asked her how she learned to cook. I've never told him that my grandfather was murdered while at work one evening.

A few minutes into the drive, he says I have an interesting family. I frown. Somehow, I never thought of my family as either interesting or boring. They're just family, which I guess can say a lot.

We reach the restaurant without him asking me about Mom's reaction. He gives me a quick kiss, says Will is picking me up after work, and he may not be home when I get back. He has to visit his family.

Chapter Twenty

A Step Forward

Leon doesn't return. His bedroom—twice as large as the cube of space I lived in—feels empty and forlorn tonight. I can't help wondering if his "family visit" is just an excuse. Could it be he has met the woman who'll be taking my place?

He comes back Sunday looking glum. I don't ask him how his visit went. The following days, Leon isn't his usual ebullient self. But he's at home asleep when I return from the restaurant.

Is our "experiment" at an end? The thought makes me sad. But I don't want to analyze why. Time enough after we part to regret what we had and where it might have taken us. I begin to scour ads for a new apartment. I have more money saved up this time so I can rent a better one.

Coming home from work Sunday night, I'm surprised to find Leon still up. He's in his pajamas and reading in bed.

He says, "Hello, beautiful. Why don't you change, get ready for bed? Put off your bath until tomorrow morning. We have to talk."

Here it is, I tell myself. The beginning of the end. I would rather relax in the tub, but I nod and drag my weary body to the dressing room.

Minutes later, we sit on the couch in a sitting area across from the foot of the bed. On the coffee table are two cold bottles of water. It may be a long night. I take one of them and begin to sip it, waiting for Leon to say something.

Leon says, "I'm not sure where to begin."

After a long moment when I say nothing, he resumes. "Okay, maybe from when I asked to visit your family."

I nod, sipping more of my water.

"Do you know why I wanted to meet them? I wanted to see what I'm getting into if we get married."

I turn toward him in surprise, trying to read his face for the truth in what he seems to be saying.

He shakes his head. "Maybe that's not a good way to begin. So, let me tell you why I went to see my family, who I must confess I visit only when I can't help it."

I stare at Leon curiously. I myself would never have thought that way about my family. But where is Leon going with his "confession"?

He scowls thoughtfully for a minute, his eyes cast down. "This house we've been living in belongs to my father, not to me. I'm paying the staff from an expense account that comes with it. He asked to see me yesterday to tell me he wants his house back."

"Leon, I'm not sure what you're really saying. If you're trying to tell me it's time for us to break up, you don't have to invent excuses. I know it's only a matter of time until it happens."

He looks at me and shakes his head. "No, that's not what I'm saying. I do have my own place. A top-floor apartment much smaller than this house, but I own it, fully paid out of my own pocket. A real estate company manages it, rents it out short-term, usually to people here on business. I can tell the agent who handles it to take it off the market."

I detect some anxiety in Leon's voice and feel sure there's a lot more he's not saying. For a moment, I regret not having given my decision to leave any more thought. But isn't this as good a time as any to decide?

I say, "Why don't we end this experiment ... this affair now? Something is bothering you that you're not telling me. Maybe you can cope better with whatever it is on your own."

"No, please, don't leave me. Actually, I'm ashamed. My father wants this house back for his new mistress. And he wants me to get out soon. When we move, we go alone. No Sara, no Luciano, although I hired them both. Will is the only one I take with me."

"Aren't you getting along with your father, Leon?"

Leon compresses his lips. Bitterly, he says, "He's an asshole. Selfish, dictatorial, cruel, and with a string of mistresses I've lost count of."

"Your mother must be a very unhappy woman."

"Not really. She has her own lover. The good thing is she's had the same one all these years. It's no longer a secret. He even gets invited to my parents' parties."

I'm dumbfounded. Leon's family sounds like characters from a soap opera. Is this the kind of freedom money brings? It's quite obvious I know zilch about the larger circle of rich people Leon is a part of.

Leon says, "Anyway, we'll have to be more self-sufficient. You need to take over the cooking, and hire the people Sara uses to clean this house to clean for us, as well. I don't know what else is needed to manage a household. You'll have to talk to Sara before we move."

"I learned more than cooking from my mom, Leon. There shouldn't be any major problems taking care of your apartment."

"That reassures me, at least. But moving out of here wasn't the only reason my father wanted to see me. He reminded me again it's time I got married. I told him I already have a fiancée and all I need to do is ask her."

"You don't mean me." I've never thought of myself as Leon's fiancée though I'm sure now he's referring to me.

"I do mean you. Do you see anyone else here at the moment? That's actually why I wanted to get acquainted with your family. I was thinking of asking you to marry me. Will you?"

"But is that really what you want?"

Leon regards me thoughtfully. "All I want is to be with you and, like I told you once, I can see spending my best years with you. I like your family, too; it feels solid. You're all so certain of each other's support and affection. But to be honest, I wouldn't want to get married. I'm being forced, for the sake of continuing the family. My father wants a legitimate heir. And soon."

"I don't know if I want to be a part of your family, Leon. I admit I've learned to love you. But is that enough? You don't want to get married, and I'm not ready. Living together was meant to be an experiment we could end any time it stopped working. When you marry, I believe you vow to make the marriage last."

"I doubt I'll ever be prepared to commit for life. You see who my role model has been. But I know at least one thing that sets me apart from my father. I won't cheat on the person I'm currently with. If I meet someone I like better, I'll break up with the previous one."

"There, you see what I mean?" I start to laugh. What he just said makes Leon's proposal even more ridiculous. "Marriage vows have a clause everyone knows about. Haven't you heard of it? Till death do us part. It's true at least half of marriages end way before death, but nobody gets married intending to divorce. But you already know that's where you're headed, maybe just a few months after the wedding."

Leon scowls. "You're leaving something out of what I said. I said 'if I meet someone I like better.' Since we've been together, I've met many women. But I've never cared for them like I care about you. You've made it hard for me to be excited about any other woman, Gina."

"Well at least that's honest, and flattering, though it's way too far from reassuring. Actually, what you need is someone to bear your child. Not a wife. Why don't you hire some woman to have your child, under the condition she marries you until he or she is born? I'm sure someone will be willing to do it for the right price."

Leon looks hurt, making me regret my crass remark. But he doesn't contradict it. "You're right, I could do that, but I want that child to be a child of love, borne from my union with a woman I love. Right now, you're that woman."

"But for how long, Leon?"

"I know you find it impossible to trust me but I trust myself. I've never been in love before but I think I love you and that's why I'm still here. And why I'm certain I'll want to be with you for a long time."

I'm either too gullible for my own good or a sentimental fool because Leon's confession of love chokes me up.

When I say nothing, Leon says, "Besides, who knows what having a son or a daughter may do for me? I've always thought it would be awesome—another person created out of one's flesh and blood. Maybe I'll want to stay with the mother of that child forever."

After a few deep breaths, I feel calmer, and what Leon said makes me say, "That precious creature will grow up in the lap of luxury and money. She would never have to struggle like I have."

"He will always be a Barrett."

Chapter Twenty-One

Brent Weighs In

On Tuesday, when my mother calls, I tell her about Leon's proposal. She says, "I don't know if I can advise you on this. In spite of myself, I like Leon. He's quite personable, has nice, easy manners. Makes you forget he's rich and privileged. But what a way to propose."

"I like how he's frank about it, though. And he's right. You can't count on things staying the way they are."

"No, you can't. Don't I know that better than most people? How one event no one ever saw coming changes your life forever? But I also know you have to work to make things happen. You're capable of that, I'm sure."

I sigh. "But you won't place your bets on Leon."

"No. But he wasn't what I expected, either."

"Well, what about the fact that our children will all be Barretts?"

"Children whose bright futures are assured. They'll have things your dad and I couldn't give you no matter how hard we worked. Can't argue against how much better it is bringing children into that world. They don't have to worry about what lies ahead for them." Is there regret in my mother's voice?

"You've given us love and your wonderful tarts."

"You'll give them those, too. If Leon can give them love, then, maybe things will work out."

I hope they will since I've run out of reasons to reject Leon's proposal.

That night, I tell Leon I'll marry him.

*****

When I see Marcia on Wednesday, I tell her Leon and I are moving to his condo and we're getting married. She's speechless for a few seconds before she says, scowling, "I didn't know he has a condo."

Bewildered, I stare at her. To me, the more important news is Leon's marriage proposal, but Marcia seems not to have heard that part. Or, she may have chosen to ignore it. So, I say, "Yes, we're moving there soon. Leon will also tell his parents he and I are getting married."

Marcia shakes her head, "His parents would never allow it."

"Leon is thirty, Marcia. Don't you think he can make his own decisions without his parents' consent?"

"Well, maybe he can. What do I really know about Leon? You've lived with him these last few months. You know him better. He has stuck with you longer than he has with anyone else."

She pauses, stares at me so intently I begin to feel uncomfortable. "Now you're marrying him. Who would have thought? Months ago, I gave you advice to just have fun with Leon while his fascination with you lasted. And look what it got you. The prize of a lifetime."

Is there envy in Marcia's voice?

She answers my unspoken question. "By the look on your face, I think you're wondering if I envy you. Of course I do. Who wouldn't jump at that chance? If Leon had asked me, I would have said yes, although I'm not in love with him."

"I do love him."

"I remember a time when you didn't want to have anything to do with him."

"He's been so sweet and patient, he won me over."

"Sweet and patient? Is that all? What about consuming passion?"

"Love comes in so many ways. Passionate love isn't always the one that lasts."

"There may be wisdom in what you say. It doesn't work for me. Anyway, when will your betrothal be announced?"

"Leon has to tell his parents first."

"Of course. When an announcement of your engagement comes out, you'll be the envy of countless women. A few will wish they could tear your heart out."

I shudder at Marcia's remarks. They bring back the image of Cristi about to strike me again with a pair of scissors. "I didn't stop to think how other women would take my marrying Leon. But there's nothing I can do about it, and it won't stop me from doing it."

"It shouldn't. Your happiness is what's important to you and it's nobody else's business."

My happiness. I can't admit to Marcia that what she said about passion and love gives me pause. Can I honestly say marrying Leon will make me the happiest of women? If marrying money and a very attractive man is the best thing that could happen to me, then I would say yes. But I'm not being honest with myself. Since accepting Leon's proposal, I have realized I don't have total control over what happens to me. I must make my choice among the alternatives fate offers me. A sad, sobering thought.

Out of the blue—or so it seems—I say to Marcia, "How's Brent?" As I ask, I feel a flutter in my breast I can't define. All these months, I've tried not to think about him, but he invades my thoughts at moments when I least want him to. Moments when the person I should be thinking about is Leon.

"Well, we're still at it. He'll be glad to hear you asked about him. He asks me about you, too. I'm sure he'll be eager to know you and Leon are getting married. Sometimes I think he takes too much interest in what's going on with you."

"I don't think Brent has any special interest in me, except as a caring friend. I haven't seen him since the dinner at your place."

"Oh, yes, I'm sure that's it. I think he is a very caring person."

"For people in general, anyway."

Frowning, Marcia stares at me thoughtfully. "Maybe that's his problem. He's incapable of relating to anyone in particular. It's lucky I've not fallen in love with him."

"Yeah, it's lucky."

"He's still an animal in bed, though, so I'm not complaining."

I shouldn't care how Brent is in bed or anywhere he cares to be, but Marcia's blathering on about him sinks me down in the dumps.

Marcia once said we're pathetic loners. Neither of us is strictly a loner now. We've become pathetic compromisers.

Three years ago, I took control of my life. Or so I thought. I was full of hope that I could go after what I want if I worked hard enough at it. But here I am, still doomed to resigning myself to choices I can't control.

I carry my regrets and melancholy back to the kitchen, but I know that in no time at all, I'll get so absorbed in what I'm doing that they'll be pushed back into a vault in my brain for things I should deal with. But only when I could.

Mom and I have been talking about the snacks Grandma used to buy every time they went to Chinatown when they were kids. Little dumplings of rice flour—pouches for all kinds of savory fillings. Shrimp, scallops, pork, chives, pea sprouts, mushrooms. The milky ice tea with gelatinous balls at the bottom that they had fun eating. I've also been learning new techniques that Guy says Laure learned working with some well-known chef in Spain. Techniques that get to the essence of food and how we experience eating. I have so much to learn. I hope to find ways to add an Asian touch to French dishes using those techniques. One day.

*****

By the end of that week, Leon and I move to his apartment. It's at a nice location with views towards the bay. Although close to a bustling commercial district, it's high up enough that noise on the streets dissipates to a faraway drone.

Up there, on the topmost floor, I feel like we're in some kind of cocoon, protected and cut off from the world. It's fine if that's what you want, but I'm discovering that isolation bothers me.

I have ranted against my old neglected neighborhood, but there, with people living so close to you, you get drawn into their lives. There's a sense of community that develops.

At Leon's father's house, I had Sara and Luciano. I tended the vegetable garden and picked flowers with Sara. On mornings when I didn't work, I went with Luciano to his favorite bakery. Sometimes, the three of us chatted over coffee around Luciano's kitchen table. I felt at ease with them, connected with them. It helped that they came from backgrounds similar to mine. But I believe what drew us closer were those moments when we did things together.

After we settle down, Leon goes home to his family again. This time, he'll tell his father he's getting married. That night, he doesn't come home.

*****

Can we meet at the Emeryville coffeehouse? This recent text message is why I now stand at ten o'clock in the morning the following day, looking for Brent in this coffeehouse. To say that I didn't expect to hear from him again doesn't come close to describing how his message affected me. The catch in my breath, the burning in my eyes as I suppress an urge to cry. Why only now, Brent?

It's the same hour I was here for the first and only time before today. I see Brent at the corner opposite where we sat before. This corner is like a living room with two low coffee tables and two loveseats arranged far enough from each other for intimate conversations. Most customers who come to this place often do work; they prefer the desk-height tables along the banquette.

He rises as I approach. I've imagined this meeting often enough in my head that I can smile casually.

"Hello, Regine," he says. He smiles but his eyes are veiled.

"Hello, Brent, it's been a while."

He picks up the two cups, one of them lidded, on the coffee table and sits down with me. He hands me the lidded cup.

"Soy milk latte for you. It should still be hot. It's only been waiting for you a minute."

I say, looking at his half-full cup, "Thank you, you remember. You drank all that whipped cream already?" I'm trying to lighten up the palpable unease we're trying to hide from each other. But it's in vain.

He smiles—barely. Finishes his coffee in one long drink. Sets the empty cup on the floor. I'm sipping my latte slowly.

"You asked me to meet you here, Brent. We haven't talked for months. Is there something you're dying to tell me?"

With knitted eyebrows, he gazes into my eyes. "Is it true you and Leon are getting married?"

"I said yes, but his parents haven't given us their consent yet."

"Gina, you know what kind of a man he is."

"You know what kind of a man Leon is, Brent?"

"I've investigated two cases that involved him. I know enough. Two women driven to assault because of how he treated them."

"Have you ever thought that maybe those two women are fragile? You can't blame Leon for what they are." I'm conscious that I'm just repeating something Leon said to me months ago.

"Maybe, but I don't think that's enough to get him off the hook. He should have been more careful who he chooses to victimize."

I agree with Brent but I chafe at the implication that I'm one of Leon's victims. "He never loved anyone before me. He told me so. Why else has he chosen to marry me?"

Brent sighs. "Maybe he does love you. But do you love him?"

"It's none of your business, isn't it? There's nothing between you and me and you have Marcia." I almost choke as I say this, swallowing tears threatening to betray me.

Brent gazes into my eyes again. "I've made a mess of this, haven't I? I thought you loved me."

I feel the tears coming. Tears of denial. Lying tears. "I can't love someone who doesn't love me. You chose Marcia."

He looks away. "Not really. It's more like I used her. Before I met you, I'd taken care not to fall in love. My work is consuming. The stress can be relentless. Worse, seeing all that violence eats at your humanity, your soul. I convinced myself commitment to a woman will only hurt both of us."

He rubs his knitted brow and glances sideways at me. "But I met you and I began to doubt my choice to devote my life to my work. Is search for justice, for truth more important than love? Can't they coexist? Do I want to spend my life alone? Am I sure I need no one? Marcia was like a sedative. She wasn't interested in a permanent relationship. She said she only wanted my body, that she couldn't live with men like me. With her, I didn't have to ask myself those agonizing questions."

"What are you trying to tell me, Brent?"

He takes my free hand in his and says, "I love you, Regine. I've loved you since that dinner at Marcia's."

Tears are threatening my composure. I shake my head. "It's too late, Brent."

I snatch my purse on the floor by my feet and bolt from the chair, out of the coffeehouse. My latte spills on my skirt but I ignore it, dumping the nearly-full cup in a trash bin outside the door. Brent calls my name, but I don't stop.

A few paces away, Brent catches up with me. Tears are now flowing down my cheeks. Tears infused with chaotic emotions. I swipe my wet cheeks with the long sleeve of my shirt.

"Regine, please don't leave like this. It hurts me to see you cry."

I stop and face him, not caring that we're on a busy street. "Why didn't you tell me you loved me that last night I called you? I was waiting for you to say so."

He shakes his head, his eyes mournful. "All I can say is I am a stupid, selfish, cowardly idiot. I knew what you wanted to hear; what you wanted me to say. I knew how I felt but I couldn't say it. My work has been the passion of my life. I couldn't just let go of it."

This time, I shake my head in regret. In sadness. In helplessness. "Can't they coexist? But you've already asked yourself, haven't you? It's too late, Brent."

"Do you love him?"

"I learned to love him. Leon is a gentleman, a charmer, an accomplished seducer of women, but he's honest. And I know he does care for me. He's shown me that."

"Am I wrong to think that you loved me once?"

"No."

"And you no longer love me."

"It doesn't matter anymore. Let's just move on." I look into his mournful eyes, touch his cheek. But he doesn't grasp my hand to kiss it like he did the night of the dinner at Marcia's. "I'll be thinking of you, Brent. Always."

I walk away, leaving Brent standing, people rushing past him.

Chapter Twenty-Two

A Mysterious Package

Why does life have to be so hard? It's not only how we choose to act that affects what happens to us. Timing, events, chance, other people. They can all change our lives. Many times, beyond our control and not to our liking.

Back home after seeing Brent, I walk around the apartment. Restless, brooding, trying not to give in to my despair. Trapped. But unwilling to hurt Leon or Marcia.

In late afternoon, the concierge at the apartment building calls me to tell me a package is waiting for me at his desk in the lobby. I'm puzzled. I've shared this address only with my family, and haven't yet given it to Laure.

But, maybe, this package comes at just the right time. I need to get away from my thoughts, the urge to cry, or kick anything within reach of my feet.

The package is small but too big for the mailbox, and a little heavy for its size. It has no return address.

I shake it and whatever is in it hardly moves. It must be an object that fits the box snugly. It has been sealed with tape on all four sides and on the center where flaps meet. Why has the sender taken care to seal the box well? Why isn't there a sender's name?

Maybe I should throw the box in the trash, unopened. But I'm more curious than afraid. And the box may just contain what I need to distract me from my blue mood. Besides, I know no one who hates me so much they'd try to harm me by mail.

I place the box on the dining table to fetch a knife. I hesitate for an instant before I slice the tape holding the flaps of the box together. What if there's something harmful in the package? But I'll never know unless I open the box, will I?

Still uneasy, I cut the tape in three quick slashes with the edge of the sharp butcher knife. When the flaps have been fully released, my worries overcome my curiosity about the contents of the package.

For a minute I stare at the top flaps, now sprung an inch at the center opening. Maybe I should wait to open it until Leon is home. The next minute, I'm convinced it's silly to think the box could contain anything dangerous.

With a flick of the knife, I push the right flap up; then I push the left. And I gasp, recoiling in surprise and disgust.

Holding my breath again, I take a step toward the box to take a closer look. Inside is a can, slightly open. Wriggling, revolting, flesh-colored worms fill the can; a few spilled onto the bottom of the box. There must be hundreds of these creatures in the can.

A note in large letters is tacked on to the inside of one flap: "Don't open this can of worms." That message is all I needed to propel me into action. Is this a joke? Whatever it is, it doesn't scare me.

I rush to the kitchen, yank a garbage bag and a pair of latex gloves from the bottom cabinet below the sink. Striding back to the dining room, I wiggle my hands into each of the two gloves.

I pick up the box by the flaps, and dump it into the bag. As I was about to twist the bag close, I decide to rip out the note. It could be evidence. Just in case. I also decide not to throw out the bag, for the same reason. But will it smell bad when the worms die in it?

Why not video the can of worms in the box? I remove the box out of the bag, pull out my cell phone, and do a forty-second video of the writhing, slithering worms.

I put the box back into the bag, twist the bag, and secure it with a tie. By the time I place it in the cabinet below the kitchen sink, my knees begin to wobble.

How bizarre. Why would a stranger bother sending a package like that to me? This experience is just plain creepy, much more disconcerting than when Leon had me followed to find out where I lived. True, it's dramatic—but it's also vague. If the sender wants to tell me not to mess with something that's likely to lead to problems, he or she would have done better to say what that something is.

I'm still a bit shaky from the can of worms when Leon arrives at the apartment at the usual time. I haven't seen him since the day before.

I wait until after dinner to tell him about the worms. He listens, frowning and pursing his lips in distaste.

"Do you want me to show you the worms and the note?"

He crinkles his nose in disgust, "No! No, I don't need to see them. I don't want to see them. I'm pretty sure they're disgusting."

"Do you think we should do something about it?"

"But what can you do? You don't know who it came from. And you can't think of anyone who hates you enough to send it. How about Cristi?"

"No, she couldn't. She's really a rather nice person." I was about to say, "and not that imaginative." But I say, "She's not capable of a cruel joke."

"It's probably just a malicious anonymous prank. Let's hope it ends there."

"Aren't you curious what the message meant— Don't open this can of worms?

"Probably just part of the prank to scare you. Clever message, though."

After I turn off my lamp to go to sleep that night, I realize the can of worms has, in fact, helped put my meeting with Brent out of my mind. It also made me forget to ask Leon how the visit with his father went.

It's too late at night to talk about it, but I nudge Leon, who's just turned off his lamp.

"What happened with your Dad today?"

"Let's talk about it tomorrow. Too tired right now." He busses me quickly on the cheek and pulls the comforter up to his shoulders.

Usually, I fall asleep soon after my head hits the pillow, but these days, I fidget a while before sleep comes. Tonight, as I close my eyes, I force myself to imagine the many dishes my future restaurant would serve. Dishes that infuse the essence of ingredients into a single bite. Maybe, I should experiment with foam. Or those tiny spheres that burst with flavor. They're like fish eggs. But they also resemble those larger balls at the bottom of the milky teas Mom had when she was a kid.

I've fallen asleep many times before while dishes on oversized plates paraded through my mind. This time, though, to my dismay, a few plates carrying squirming worms follow rice dumplings filled with salmon and spinach. Then, I find myself lying on a bed full of slithering worms. They're strangely cool and velvety against my skin. Not entirely unpleasant.

I try to get up from bed, but my body feels too heavy. So, I scream. Brent will hear me, I'm sure, and pull me out of these worms. Here he is, calling my name and placing his arm around me. What took you so long?

I open my eyes and stare at Leon's face. "Shhh. You had a nightmare."

Snuggling closer to Leon, I say in a quivering voice, "I'm sorry to wake you up." My words end in a sob I can't suppress.

"It's okay. Go back to sleep."

But the images from the dream make me shudder and keep me awake for a couple of hours.

The next morning at breakfast, Leon tells me his father isn't happy about us getting married. Lines are etched deeper on his forehead and he's clenching his jaw. "That's how I expected him to react. He has this need to control my whole life. If I let him, he'll dictate exactly who I'll marry."

"Maybe we shouldn't go through with it."

"No, we'll go ahead with it, with or without his consent. I'm betting his desire for an heir is stronger than his impulse to control me."

"Don't you think it's better if he gives us his blessing?"

"I'll try one more time. I think I should bring you home to dinner. He might change his mind. He likes beautiful women and he's a gourmand."

*****

"I got a weird package in the mail two days ago," I say to Marcia on Wednesday.

"Why? What's in in it?"

"A can of worms."

"What do you mean a can of worms?" She's frowning and chuckling at the same time.

"A can of worms. You know, those long, tiny, slimy, wriggly creatures you find in your garden."

"That's bizarre. Who was it from?"

"Don't know. No return address. Leon thinks it's a prank."

"Could be. Anything in the package to give you a clue who it's from?"

"No, but there's a note: 'Don't open this can of worms.'"

Marcia smiles with relish. "Clever metaphor. Must be some nerd having malicious fun. I bet he sent those cans to a number of people."

Minutes later, as we're returning to our work stations, she says, "Anything you've done recently that you think may cause trouble for you?"

"No. Why?"

"You sure?"

I shake my head. "I'm sure. Nothing new."

"You're thinking of getting married to a guy who's every other girl's dream. That's new. One of those girls might be envious enough to send you this package as a message."

"I didn't think of that. But it's possible. Leon's ex-girlfriends have done crazy things."

"You've already been a victim of one. By a best friend, at that. Be careful, okay?"

A larger package arrives a few days later, sealed all over like the first one was. My first impulse is to throw it, without opening it, into the bag with the first box. But again, my curiosity gets the better of me. The box is bigger, so something else must be in it. If it's just more worms, I'll survive. With a few slashes of the butcher knife, I release the flaps on the box.

Except for the size, this box is a repeat of the first, with a bigger can of worms. Same note. Why bother sending me a second one? In disgust, I slam the flaps together and dump the box into the bag with the first.

This time, I don't tell Leon about the second. He'll explain it like the first—a joke from a prankster who has nothing better to do. Maybe he's right.

But what if Marcia is right? Some girl out there, someone I don't know, may be sending me a warning. After what Cristi did to me, the idea creeps me out. Still, only people close to me and who I trust know Leon and I plan to get married.

I shove the bag under the sink, twisted on top and tied securely to prevent stinky odors from escaping.

That night, I dream, not of the worms, but of running after Brent and Marcia. Marcia's face alternating with Cristi's. The dream is old. It has recurred twice before.

Chapter Twenty-Three

The Experiment Ends

What do you think I should wear to dinner with Leon's parents?" I ask Marcia, as we sit once again on crates at the back of Du Cœur.

Her head jerks toward me, a look of surprise in her eyes. "Are you there already? Has his father said yes?"

"No, but Leon thinks his father will say yes if I meet him, so I need to make a good impression."

"Will it be at their house in Los Altos?"

"As far as I know."

She knits her forehead and looks away. "Something nicer than what you'd wear in an office. Be yourself and don't let him intimidate you. I think his father likes to do that."

It's my turn to look at Marcia in surprise. "Have you met Leon's father?"

"No. I've only seen him here the few times he came with Leon. But I hear things. When's your dinner?"

"I hope sometime this month. Seems even dinners need to be put on his official schedule. Leon will talk to him this week."

Marcia snickers and pats my knee. "This dinner may decide your fate, but try to have fun. I hear they have a great personal chef."

*****

Life at the condo has settled to a routine. On Mondays, I do some tidying up. Cleaners come on Tuesdays. Without Luciano to cook for Leon, I also prepare some dishes for his frequent solitary dinners.

It amazes me how patient he can be for a pampered brat who's always had someone at his beck and call, who's used to getting what he wants when he wants it. But it's early yet. We've only been by ourselves a few weeks. And I make and plate his dinner so he only needs to microwave it. I can also rely on him to put his dirty dishes in the dishwasher.

On Monday, towards the end of breakfast, Leon puts a hand on mine as I'm about to get up to place dirty dishes in the sink. "Stay. We need to talk."

"Aren't you going to work? It's past nine," I say.

"No, they know I won't be in this morning."

There is something in his voice that bothers me. A gravity I'm not accustomed to. A quietness that often comes with bad news.

He looks down at his cup, rubbing one side of it back and forth with his fingers. I'm more certain now he's going to say something about to change things drastically for the two of us.

"What is it Leon?"

"Gina, this is very hard for me ...." The crease in Leon's knitted brow deepens and his eyes narrow in suppressed anger.

"I know. I'll wait until you're ready. I'm not going anywhere."

He stares back at me. "What do you mean you know?"

"Well, I've seen that look in your eyes. You get it when you talk about your father. I think you've seen him. I guess he doesn't want to have me over to dinner at your family home."

"Yes, we talked, twice. I don't know why I keep trying." His gaze returns to his cup of coffee. "He's a bastard."

"That's no way to talk about your father, Leon."

"Well, he is a bastard. And he plays that role with relish. He knows his money gives him the power to be as much of an asshole as he wants, and get away with it."

"What exactly did he tell you?"

"He says he doesn't need to meet you, that he's never going to give his consent."

"But we knew that already. Something else must have happened. That's why you're so angry."

Leon sighs, still staring at his cup. He pushes it violently away. I stop it with my hand to prevent it from crashing on the floor. He bolts out of his chair and turns around, his back to me. He stands motionless for a long moment, his hands clenched, his body as taut as a line tied too tightly at both ends.

Staring at Leon's rigid back is like butting against a concrete wall at the end of a street. There's no way forward. I've been forewarned, but I've learned to love Leon and I'm sorry it has to end just when we've agreed to move on to a more committed relationship. Still, when I look back on these past months, it's losing Brent that I've regretted most.

Finally, Leon finds his voice again. "He had his private investigator .... He knows who you are. The second time we talked, he threatened to cut me out of his will, out of everything the Barretts have stood for if I don't do as he says."

His eyes blazing with anger, he turns to face me again. "He will take away from me a legacy due me as the oldest son. That's the way it's always been. This legacy belongs to me and nobody else's. Not even my younger brother."

He paces back and forth from one end of the room to the other. "He's groomed me to take over the Barrett fortune and everything Barretts have stood for. I've played along, taking in every unpleasant thing he threw at me without complaining. I could have rebelled. I was tempted to, many times. But I understood: The Barrett legacy has to be kept alive and the responsibility falls on me. My brother can do what he wants, but not me. He was molding me to inherit his role. And his image."

He bangs his palm on the table. "I hate that image! But he taught me well. And sometimes I hate myself."

"But you're not cruel, Leon."

"No? You once said I was an asshole."

"I also said you're sweet and thoughtful. I also know you better now and maybe, I can even understand why you change girlfriends so often. But the image of your father—and you—which you find so hateful—it doesn't have to be part of that legacy, does it?"

"No. I've told myself many times it's for me to change that image. That I wouldn't want my son to grow up like my father. Or like me."

For the first time, I feel a deep sympathy for Leon. If I had seen this side of him early on—one I can't yet define in the swirl of emotions between us—could I have loved him as deeply as I've loved Brent?

He resumes pacing, faster at first. But he slows down and his voice is quieter when he speaks again. "I do love you, Gina. With the others, it was all about sex and having a good time. But with you ... you may be right that it was lust when I first saw you at Du Cœur, but you touched me, tugged at my heart from the start."

He stops in front of me. "I love you but I can't let my father take my legacy away from me. I've invested too much in it, suffered for it."

Leon kneels on the floor and takes me in his arms. "I hope you understand."

Tears begin to roll down my cheeks as I put my arms around him. "I can sympathize with your agony, Leon, though I can't understand how a legacy can mean so much to anyone."

No, I can't grasp the hold a legacy has on people like Leon. The weight it puts not only on his shoulders, but also in his spirit. Just as I couldn't fully fathom Brent's anguished preoccupation with justice and getting at the root of why people kill.

I realize, in a vague way, that the burden of legacy and knowing why people kill are as far apart as can be, but I think I understand passion, and both Brent and Leon possess it. Adam, my first boyfriend, didn't. He was merely following a path laid out for someone like him. Not that it's wrong to do so. But to me, there's something noble about passion for something that's outside of yourself; that's bigger than yourself. How else can we elevate life from the ordinary?

Leon and I hold each other for a long while. Neither of us says anything more. Nothing more needs to be said. We quietly accept the burden that will soon tear us apart for good.

He doesn't go to work that afternoon. We decide to drive towards the coast and along it, as far north as the late September light would let us. We don't talk much. Leon has opened the car windows and the skylight, and we get lost in the cacophony that surrounds us. The car engine's low hum. The occasional squawking of sea gulls. Gentle waves lapping on sandy shores sometimes broken by violent waves slapping on rocks. Dissonances that drown Leon's anguish and my sorrow.

We stay at a roadside inn that evening. At dinnertime, we go to a restaurant the hotel manager tells us serves fish fresh off the fishing boats that day. The simply-grilled fish complimented by fries prepared from scratch lift our spirits a bit.

That night, we hold each other, but we don't make love. The bed is firm and uncomfortable for Leon. Sleep claims my consciousness without effort. Hurting and anguish can take at least as much out of you as physical labor. In those periods of light sleep, I sense Leon turning and tossing next to me.

Back at Du Cœur, the gravity of Leon's mood stays with me. Is it because loss is so personal that you can't share it with other people? But Marcia doesn't seem to notice my silence. She's stopped talking about Brent, and I think she has her own concerns she prefers not to share with me. So, during break, we walk and make small talk.

*****

Leon and I have to part. And soon. As much as this recent crisis has drawn us closer together, I'm aware that the longer I stay with him, the deeper leaving will hurt. But he doesn't say anything about me leaving, nor has he made any move to hint that I should go. I think we were getting used to each other's company. Maybe that's part of how love can last. The comfort of familiarity. The reassurance and the quiet acceptance that come with it.

I tell myself I must begin the process of ending our little experiment. We'll both need to get back to the business of mundane daily living. I need to find a new apartment. This time, I can get a better one because I'm making more money than when I started my first cooking job. I have also saved up a few thousands from the months of living with Leon.

One morning, at breakfast, before we both go to our jobs, I bring the matter up.

"I have to move out soon, Leon. I've been looking for a new apartment and found one I'd like to check out."

Leon looks up from his coffee and says, "No, don't do that. I'll move out. You stay here. I'm pretty sure I can go back to the Claremont Hills house because my father seems to have tired of his current mistress pretty fast. He'll kick her out soon."

"I don't want charity, Leon," I say with some vehemence. I take offense that he thinks he should "pay" me in some way for having lived with him.

"Gina, please. Don't get me wrong. This isn't charity or payment. I want to give you something of me. Something that can last. Unfortunately, this is all I have right now that I fully own, that I worked for to get. I have transferred the title of this condo to you."

I stare at him, surprised at first; then, quickly, I scowl in dismay, "No, Leon! I can't accept it. I won't."

"You must, because if you don't, taxes won't get paid, and the city will seize this property. It will be lost. So, you see, you're not going to own it without responsibility. You'll have to pay $15,000 annual property taxes, but I figure you can do that on your salary. There are utility bills to pay, but since you're by yourself, it's not much more than you might pay if you rent an apartment."

I shake my head. "You've thought about all this, haven't you?"

"Yes, I had a lot to sort out."

"Why are you doing this Leon?"

"I'm not quite sure why. I just know I want to. Maybe I'm trying to alleviate my remorse. Maybe I don't want you to ever forget me. I bought this condo to live in away from my family and before my father enticed me with the house on the Hills. This place means a lot to me. It's a haven. It means freedom. You're the first woman I've ever truly cared for. I never thought I was capable of that. In learning how to care for someone else, I feel like I've also been set free."

How depressing it is to hear Leon talk like that. I always thought his money gave him freedom most people wished they had. But it seems he is shackled by that money and the kind of person he has become because of it. I suppose it should make me feel good if it's true that, in some little way, I have freed him from the shackles of money and legacy. But doesn't every person have a natural ability to care or love someone else? Caring isn't something you buy or trade for a legacy.

Leon's lips twitch, in an attempt to smile. "Don't look so sorry and sad for me. In choosing my legacy, I'm giving you up and selling my soul to my father, but I'll have an obscene amount of money that will last a few lifetimes. I can easily get another haven like this one. Larger and more luxurious."

"But your choice is making you so unhappy."

Leon sighs. When he speaks, I sense an ominous note in his voice. "This is my destiny, I'm afraid. My father will get what he wants of me, but I'll make him pay an exorbitant price."

"I don't think I'll ever understand you, Leon. It seems to me you're giving in to him, but you're also thinking of getting back at him for it."

He doesn't answer right away. He's clenching his teeth, and that look of suppressed anger brightens his eyes once again. Then with a sneer, he says, "That's how it's always been between the two of us. But I'll win in the end. I'll outlast him for sure. And he'll leave a fortune that I can do with as I please. I know that bugs him like nothing else does. He'd take his money to the grave if he could."

What could I say to words that speak of hate and revenge? I avert my eyes down to my hands, clasped together on top of the table. We sit in silence. Silence suits us. Soothes us. The Leon I had known was uneasy in silence. He broke it with words, with action.

It's my turn to break it. Not because I'm uneasy, but because I think: Why not accept what he's offering? I'll never forget him. I don't want to forget him. But I'm also practical. I doubt I can afford to keep this pricey piece of memory he's offering me as his legacy.

"What if I take this place and sell it?"

"It's yours. You can do what you want with it. Rent it, sell it, use the money to open that restaurant you've always dreamed of owning. All I want is for you not to forget me, to always remember I helped you make your dreams come true. That's really what means a lot to me—to know that I made a difference in your life. A difference in the life of the only woman who's ever really touched me. Who's freed me up in some way from my family. I suppose, in a way, it's a sort of legacy I'm leaving you."

A few days later, Leon is gone.

Exactly what I'll do with his legacy, I haven't decided yet. All I know is I can't afford to live in it. Maintaining it means I have much less (or none at all) to put into the pot I'm saving for that distant future when I can open my own restaurant. Besides, it seems so lonely living too far away from where you see life, hear it, taste it, be a part of the chaos it can become every day.

I miss Leon. We've agreed to cut all ties to make it easier on both of us. But on days when I'm not at work, I half expect him to call me to tell me he's found a hole-in-the-wall we should try out for lunch.

Before he walked out the door on the day he left, I kissed him all over his face. "I'll never forget you, Leon and I won't want to."

He held me tight for a long time, then he said, "I'll miss you, Gina. I'll miss your passion. Your refreshing innocence. The fact that you taught me I can love. But I can't help who I am."

Chapter Twenty-Four

Mysterious Mail

Is it strange that loss can make you reluctant to share your feelings and thoughts with another, even your best friend and your mother? But maybe that's just me. I haven't told anyone that it's over between Leon and me.

I'm conscious that, nowadays, something about me is quieter. I talk less, force my smiles, and seek quiet things—soft music, books and movies about women searching for themselves, pictures of solitary figures and calm nature scenes. It's a new state of being that I find I'm comfortable with. But I haven't lost my enthusiasm for concocting new and tasty dishes. I come alive at the kitchen in Du Cœur. It's the source of my pleasure. The salve to heal my bruised self. The food my spirit craves. As I give myself fully to this act of creating dishes that nourish others, I also feed my soul.

As is my habit, I check my snail mailbox for letters before I go to work. These days, it's Leon's mailbox. I suppose it's mine now. But no one will be sending me any mail here. No one but my family has this address. And no one in my family is a letter-writer. Leon asked me to forward any mail that looks important to the house on the Hills.

Today, one stands out from the rest. It's in a pink squarish envelope and fragrance seeps out of it. My first thought: An old flame. A new one? If so, Leon isn't wasting any time. But the letter is addressed to me. Who could it have come from?

I open it as soon as I get into my car. It's brief, and very word on the pink page raises goose bumps:

Get out of Leon's apartment. You're in serious danger.

What does this mean? Is it a hoax like the cans of worms? Two boxes and a letter sent to me, all with threatening messages—can someone keep up that kind of hoax? And does that person have any intention of following up on it? But who would do such a thing?

I get sick to my stomach that someone out there has thought to do me serious harm. It's happened once already, though Cristi acted on the spur of the moment. The person sending me these threatening messages may have been planning to hurt me for some time. Does she hate me so much she wants to kill me?

I shudder thinking about it. But I tell myself I can't dwell on the message in the pink letter. Du Cœur is waiting. It's time to make things that give pleasure, that give life. No time to waste on messages calculated to instill fear and provoke, but that may not be acted upon.

My forced nonchalance is brief, and it takes me a few moments to turn the key on the ignition. I force my leaden foot to step on the accelerator, to steer it out of its parking space.

I can't just ignore the letter. The message with the cans of worms? Maybe too vague. This last one? Scary. Enough to make me dread going to my empty home tonight. No place else to go, though. A cheap hotel room, maybe?

Meantime, I have to put my worries on hold until I leave Du Cœur. I'll ask Laure if she can release me an hour before dinner service ends.

Urgent personal business, I say before she can answer. If she doubts my excuse, she doesn't show it.

When the hour comes, I sit in my car in the parking lot, googling for a cheap hotel on my cellphone. But as I start to dial the number of a prospective hotel, I realize I have a more urgent need than finding a bed for a night or more.

The pink letter—I must deal with it first. Isn't it why I'm frantically searching for a hotel room?

I need help. If nothing else, I should talk to someone at the police station tomorrow morning before I go to work.

But why not Brent? I know he can help me figure this out. But can I ask him? Our last meeting had been unpleasant and meeting again would be awkward, to say the least. Was that less than a month ago?

Anyway, he's in homicide. Dealing with this cryptic message isn't his department. But, he's a friend, despite that last meeting. He won't turn me away.

I call Brent's number before I argue against myself again. The phone rings twice, and stops. Words spill out of my mouth in a trembling rush. "I'm sorry to call you this late, but I'm scared."

It takes him a moment to answer. Maybe he never expected to hear from me again. When he answers, his voice seems as agitated as mine. "Gina? What's wrong?"

"A threat. In a letter. I can't go back to Leon's... to my apartment."

Another pause. Maybe, I'm not making sense to him. I know I'm not making much sense to myself. But he answers. "Why? Did Leon threaten you? Is he home?"

"No, no. He's gone. It's all over. It's a pink letter in the mail. I don't know what to do."

"What does the letter say?"

"Get out of Leon's apartment. You're in serious danger." The words quiver out of my mouth, my teeth knocking against each other.

"Where are you?"

I take a moment to calm myself. "At the restaurant parking lot."

"Can you drive? Come to my house?"

"Where's your house? But I don't want to be any trouble to you."

"No, you won't. You're a friend in need, right? What are friends for? Anyway, we'll have to find out what that note means. We can do it better face-to-face. And I can also put you up for tonight at least, if you're scared to go home."

Fifteen minutes and ten miles later, I knock on Brent's door.

He opens it right away, dressed in a robe and pajama bottoms. "Regine," he says, in that soft—now achingly sweet—way he's always uttered my given name. "Come in."

My anguish, the mournfulness in his eyes at our last meeting make me hesitate on his doorstep. But I'm also shivering, and now that we're standing face-to-face, I'm near tears. "I'm sorry to disturb you this late, but I didn't know what else to do."

With that ever-so-slight smile and a shake of his head, he says, "Please don't worry. I'm a night owl, as you know. The truth is I'm quite happy to see you. I hoped, but I never expected it to be this soon."

His hand on my back, he ushers me into his small living room and on to his couch. "You look beat. A glass of warm milk?"

"Yes, yes, I think so." It's all I can think of to say as I begin to wonder, sitting on the large couch in his warm living room, if I should even be here, regretting for a few moments that I came. What if Marcia drops into his house tonight?

Brent brings me milk he microwaved in a coffee cup, hands it to me without a word, and sits next to me on the couch. He's silent, watching me as I drink.

Nervous, tired, and hungry, I finish the milk a little too quickly. Brent takes the empty cup from me and places it on the table on his side of the couch. He says, "Now, tell me about the letter."

"It came in the mailbox this morning. Except for my mother, I've never given that address to anyone." I pull the pink letter out of my backpack. I drop it on his cupped hand as if it's a match with the flame reaching the end of its stick.

He sniffs the envelope. "I think that's a woman's perfume or cologne." He scowls. "A bit familiar. Probably popular. But not cheap."

He takes the letter out, glances at the printed content. "Is this the first one you received?"

"Yes, but not too long ago, I also got two boxes with cans of worms in them. They had no return addresses and Leon thought they might have been a random hoax. They came with a message. The same one: 'Don't open this can of worms.' Now, I think they're not a hoax, not after that pink letter."

"We'll have to see. They may amount to nothing. But you never know. Anyway, you really look like you need to sleep. So if you can relax, I say let's put this off for tomorrow."

"I can relax. You're right. I'm exhausted. Maybe all this will prove to be another hoax tomorrow."

"I'll take you to the guest room. The bed is made. There are fresh towels in the bathroom. How about I lend you a pajama top?"

I nod, allow myself to be led, and utter a feeble, "Thank you."

Five minutes later, I'm in the shower, relishing the warmth of the water flowing down my body. Thinking, Brent is just a door from me.

Chapter Twenty-Five

Brent

Clutching the towel, already damp from the beads of water on my body, I sit on the bed, seeing the room for the first time. After the large spaces and expensive furniture in the Hills house and Leon's condo, this small spare room is comforting, embracing. Nothing in it is superfluous. A bed that's firm, but yielding under my weight, a nightstand, a chair and writing table, and two lamps, one on each table. Except for the white bed covers, everything is a soft shade of olive green.

I bring the damp towel to my wet head, rubbing slowly at first, then vigorously. Grabbing a handful of hair, I shake off countless droplets of water. I could use a hair dryer. Maybe I should ask Brent to lend me one. He's just a door away. The thought of it mesmerizes me.

What happens next is a blur, like stepping into a dream sequence belonging to someone else. Maybe it's fatigue; maybe it's all the events of the past weeks, over which I had no control, events to which I was a mere spectator, but one who absorbed the pain I witnessed.

Wrapping the damp towel around my body, I get up. I don't walk; I float, borne by a warm breeze. It sets me down just outside Brent's room, where I stand for a few moments. His door is ajar and I open it wide. Slowly, I take a few steps in, and stand gazing at him under the white sheets. Maybe he's asleep.

But he isn't. Lifting his head off his pillow, he says, "Regine?"

I say nothing, let the towel fall slowly to the floor as I glide toward the bed. I crawl into bed with him. He lifts the sheets and makes room for me. He wraps me in the sheets, puts an arm around me and says, "Go to sleep. You're safe here with me."

What a strange thing to say: Go to sleep. You're safe...

I turn toward him, pull his face to mine, and press my lips to his.

He returns my kiss, but follows it with those strange words again: "Go to sleep. You're all stressed out."

With a sob, I say, "Make love to me. Why can't you? Have your feelings changed so quickly?"

"Oh, Regine, my love, is that really what you want?"

"Yes, more than anything. I've waited too long."

He moves and, for an instant, I'm afraid he'll get up and escort me back to the guest room like a small child.

Instead, I feel his lips nibbling around my neck, moving up my chin, then sucking at my lower lip.

I cling to him, answering his every kiss with an intensity I haven't experienced before.

His lips wander down my neck, lingers on my breasts for a while. He stops, and I suppress a cry in protest.

He kicks off the sheet and flings his pajama bottoms on the floor.

He crouches above me, his hands caressing every part of me, his lips searing the skin all over my body. He says, "You're trembling."

"No more than you." I say, stroking his chest and his stomach, kneading the muscles in his arms. Brent is sinewy; every muscle in his body ripples with strength.

My hand wanders down, grasping him. He utters a groan, a fusing of pleasure and pain.

Moaning, I pull him closer. "I want you in me."

He positions himself between my legs, and bends over to take my mouth in his. He thrusts into me slowly, deeply, a long, drawn-out breath escaping his mouth. He stops for a few seconds. I feel him throbbing and a moan rises out of my chest.

He says in a soft voice, "Don't move, not yet."

Seconds later, he resumes thrusting at a slow steady pace.

Leaning on his elbows, he lies on top me and murmurs into my ear. "I've longed to make love to you for so long. Many nights before I go to bed, I imagine doing this, but it's never as delicious as this."

I run my hands up and down his back and say nothing, relishing his rhythmic movement inside me.

He murmurs into my ear again, "I don't want this to end. Is this real and not a dream? Are you actually here, and I'm making love to you?"

I pull his head down and suck on his lower lip. I say huskily, "Is that real enough for you?"

"Oh my love," he says as he presses harder on my lips and increases the pace of his movement.

I grab his buttocks, pushing him deeper into me, our bodies rocking in wondrous synchrony.

I can't say when the dream ended. The next thing I remember is waking up in the morning from a tender kiss on my cheek and the smell of coffee on my nose. I open my eyes to look up at Brent's smiling face.

Reaching down under the sheets, I touch my naked skin and the moist spot between my legs. I can still feel him inside me.

Brent is smiling at me. A tender, relaxed smile that floods his face with a glow as warm as moonlight. "Good morning. It's early, but I'd like us to go to your apartment to check it out before you go to work; maybe even get someone to change your locks. You shouldn't have to feel scared in your own home."

"Good morning," I say, blushing.

"Do you regret last night?"

"No, how could I? It was beautiful. Like a magical dream. Was it real?" I smile back at him.

He plants a soft kiss on my lips. "I'll always be here when you need me, Regine. I want you to know that. Always."

That night, I return to the apartment. Brent went through it in the morning, checking and finding nothing suspicious. He stayed until the locksmith he called had changed the locks while I went to work. He came to Du Cœur just before it opened for dining, gave me my new keys, and whispered that he'd see me again soon.

I pressed a new key in his hand. "Just in case," I say.

He smiled, shoving the key in his pants pocket. "Are we still in your magical dream?"

"Dream. Reality. Does it really matter? I'm happy is all I know."

He kissed my hand, then my lips, before he sauntered away.

I passed the day calm, giddy, and incredulous. A day that started in fear ended bringing Brent and me back together.

Chapter Twenty-Six

Marcia Makes Her Move

It's Monday and Du Cœur is closed. Brent has texted me a few times. He's been busy on a new homicide case, and I haven't seen him for a few days.

Yesterday, he sent me a text. He'll come by my apartment late this afternoon.

Shortly before noon, the doorbell rings. I couldn't believe he's here already, but I rush to let him in. I was about to unlock the door when I remember Brent warning me to be more cautious. I peek through the peephole, and can't quite believe my eyes—Marcia in a red dress, holding a small white box, the kind bakeries pack pastries in.

"Marcia!" I say, both pleased and puzzled. "Come in."

We buzz each other's cheeks, and I lead her to the couch. "How did you find this place?"

"You never gave me the address, so I asked Leon."

"Did he tell you?"

"Tell me what?"

"That the marriage is off."

She stares at me, incredulous. "No, he said nothing."

As I sit down next to her, she says, "I hate to say I told you so. I knew his father wouldn't give his consent."

"Just goes to show you how naïve I am. Leon was sure he could convince his father and I believed him."

"That's Leon. He can make anyone—including himself—believe anything. But I'm disappointed you never told me."

"I guess our breakup affected me more than I ever thought it would. You're the one who said I should just have fun with him. And I did. Still, I was prepared for the relationship to end after a few months. I did develop some affection for him, and these last couple of weeks, I saw a side of him that surprised me. A side that made me love him. But I never thought he'd propose. I sure didn't expect it."

"Well, I guess you never know when love can hit you. I would never have bet on Leon falling for anyone. And to ask you to live with him—never crossed my mind. Then, he gives you this place."

"Did Leon tell you that?"

"Not really. I assumed it's his wedding present to you."

"But why would you think that? I don't understand why Leon didn't tell you the marriage is off."

"Maybe he forgot."

"He transferred this place in my name without asking me. I would have protested if I had known. It's too much."

"Gina, you don't have to apologize or feel guilty for accepting it. It's only right he should atone for breaking your engagement. I think it also shows his appreciation for the time he spent with you. Leon is nice and generous that way. And you deserve it."

"Thank you for saying so. It makes me feel better. I wish I could keep it, but I can't. Can't afford it. Not if I have to save for that dream restaurant."

"No, you can't keep it. Still, lucky you. Thinking of selling it?"

"In time. I have a few months yet. The taxes would eat up my yearly savings, but they're paid this year."

"Sell it, then your dreams can come true much sooner."

After her reassuring words, Marcia lapses into silence, and I remember my obligations as a hostess. "Coffee or tea?" I say, getting up from the couch.

Marcia looks up at me, but something in her expression has changed. She's looking at me, but her unfocused gaze tells me her mind has wandered off elsewhere.

"Marcia," I say, my voice louder. "Coffee or tea?"

"Oh, uhh, coffee. Black." Then, remembering the box she brought with her, she picks it up off the coffee table where she had placed it. "I brought us some cookies to nibble on. Bitter dark chocolate."

I pick up the box, but before I reach the kitchen, I look back at her. She's sitting upright, her body rigid, and she's clutching something in her hand.

Five minutes later, I return, carrying a tray with two small cups, a pot of espresso-maker coffee, and a plate of Marcia's chocolate cookies.

She says, frowning, "Espresso cups may not be a good idea."

"I'll get you a bigger cup, if you want."

"No, maybe this will work. No, you're right. Get a bigger cup."

I walk slowly back to the kitchen, struck by Marcia's sudden, strange behavior—*she's distracted and being weird about the coffee cup*. A feeling of apprehension creeps up my chest. What is going on? How can her mood change while I was making coffee?

Uneasy, I return to the living room. As I put the cup down on the table, Marcia pulls at my arm. "Sit down and fill that cup with coffee."

I sit but my gaze doesn't stray away from Marcia's face. Something is definitely wrong. I stare at the glazed look in her eyes—and realize I've seen it before. On Cristi, just before she attacked me. Like an icy wind, a feeling of dread hits me, making me shudder for a moment.

I gingerly move a few inches away from Marcia, hoping she won't notice. As I pour coffee in the big cup, I stare down at her hand that's holding something. It's a bottle.

She places it on the table, and I see it's filled with pills. She says, "Pick it up and open it."

I ignore her command and try to act like I'm in control. "What's going on, Marcia? Are you sick?" It reassures me that my voice sounds steady enough.

"Yes, but not in the way you may be imagining."

"Can you tell me what's wrong?"

"What's wrong? Are you really that dense? Yes, I'm sick. Sick of how things are. Sick of how certain people have these advantages. This luck." Venom coats every word spitting out of her mouth.

She glares at me with narrowed eyes. "You know, Leon helped me buy my condo. But I had to pay mortgage and taxes from day one. You, you open your legs and you get all these, free and clear. Then, there's Brent. Open the bottle."

This time, I pick up the bottle and glance at the label. The icy wind has seeped into my blood, coursing through my whole body. I take in a deep breath and with feigned disbelief, I say, "Marcia, what are you doing? These pills. You're not taking them. I won't let you."

"If you think I'm going to kill myself because I'm sick of being the loser, you're wrong."

I make a motion to get up from the couch, but Marcia's hand restrains me and her other hand reaches for something behind her on the couch. She points a gun at me.

"The contents are for you. Bitch! You've taken things from me long enough."

"Marcia, I don't understand. Leon and I are through."

"It's not just Leon. Brent, too."

"But you said he was just a fling."

"He made it clear from the beginning he was in love with another woman. So, I told him sex was all I was after. That like him, I couldn't afford to have a relationship."

"Oh, Marcia, I'm so sorry."

"Are you? It didn't take long for me to realize Brent meant you. But why you? Because you're young? Pretty?

Don't a good mind and a giving heart mean anything anymore?"

My lips begin to quiver, but I can't show Marcia I'm scared. I purse my lips, take another deep breath, and I glare at her. "I want you to leave now, Marcia. Please go. I'll forget this ever happened."

"You're not going to get off that easy."

"Brent is on his way here."

"Ahh, Brent! Didn't take you long, did it? As soon as Leon left, you went after your next prey."

"You got it all wrong." The truth hits me then. My voice cold with both fear and incredulity, I say, "The cans of worms, the pink letter. They all came from you. You followed me to get this address. You didn't talk to Leon."

"Voila! Catching on, at last. Can't say I didn't warn you. But you're so thick-headed you ignored them."

"I didn't. Your pink letter is why I went to see Brent. He's coming to tell me what he found."

Marcia shakes her head and sneers. "You think that will stop me? I'm way too deep in this already. Brent is as big a bastard as Leon. I thought he was different. They think I'm old and fat but they have no shame having sex with me, taking what they can from me."

"You know you can't get away with this."

"I know. I don't care. But you'll go before I go. Take your pick. A gun is much quicker but it's messy. Besides, if you mess up this apartment with blood and murder, you'll have—I mean your parents—will have trouble selling it and it won't be worth much. Your dying won't help anyone. A suicide can be kept hush-hush."

"Marcia, please don't do this."

She glares at me and shouts, "Open the bottle and swallow everything. Don't make me shoot because, by God, I will."

My cold hands unscrew the bottle. *I have a better chance surviving a bottle of sleeping pills than a gun.* Those are my thoughts as I stuff the pills in my mouth. Some drop on the couch, but Marcia doesn't seem to care.

I'm gagging on the pills, and Marcia shoves the cup of coffee towards me. "Drink. All of it."

I swallow the coffee, gagging a couple more times. Thinking, hoping in the thickening haze in my brain that the caffeine would lessen the effect of the pills. Marcia seizes the cup from my hand, puts it down on the table.

I say, "I'm so sorry for you, Marcia. You're a better person than this."

Slowly slumping on the couch, my vision begins to blur, but I keep my eyes focused on Marcia. I murmur: "You can't kill me that easily."

Marcia pries the bottle out of my hand, but gathering whatever strength I have left. I don't let go. As my consciousness slowly fades, a ghostly image of her flashes before my eyes, and I think: *she's frightened.*

She jerks herself up from the couch, and in a shaky voice, she says, "Gina, I'm so sorry."

All those words Marcia has uttered today—I resolve to remember them. It may take me months, years to recover and fully heal, but I will never forget. I'm sure I would look upon those words with anger at her, at myself. But underneath that anger, there would be disgust for allowing myself to be betrayed. And yet, I doubt that I could have known it would come to this.

I no longer have the strength to keep my eyelids open, though I can still hear muffled steps going farther away, disappearing.

Suddenly, a loud bang jolts me out of oblivion. But only for an instant.

Epilogue

What a relief! The lunch hour rush has finally eased up, and I'm in need of a little self-care. I flex my back and arm muscles twice before I sit at my desk in the fifty-square-foot space that passes for my office. I glance at the window behind my chair to check if it's open. It brings in sunlight and fresh air, and keeps me from feeling hemmed in. I listen for a moment to the hum of the large temperature-controlled pantry four feet in front of my desk that lends some cool air to the room.

Three years ago, I would never have predicted I'd be here in my own office, running my version of a French deli. Upon release from the hospital for overdosing on sleeping pills, I slowly recovered, largely with my mother's help. It wasn't so much my body as it was my mind and my spirit that needed to heal, and looking around this warehouse-like room behind the storefront, I'd say I'm doing just fine.

I still have to work on resuscitating my trust in people. I do pretty well, though, with teens and young adults. And my family, of course. Without their help, recovery would have been a long struggle up a steep peak, and this French deli would have remained a dream.

After five minutes of sitting still and focusing on my breathing, I pick up the stack of snail mail on my desk and sift through advertisements, solicitations, and business letters, searching for an envelope from the university. *Et, voila, c'est ici* (it's here). With a letter opener, I rip the top of the envelope, quickly scanning its contents: Three "As" and a "B." As I expected. At the rate I'm going, I'll get my degree in two and a half years; three, if I can't take the courses I need.

Business is picking up. But I prefer to expand my possibilities, so I'm working on a bachelor's degree in food science, with a minor in French. I'll be striding towards thirty by the time I graduate.

A year into my recovery, the building that housed my grandfather's deli went on sale. To me, it seemed like an omen, and I decided to take full control of my fate. The decision marked the beginning of a new phase in my life and the rebirth of my dreams.

I sold Leon's condo and bought the small two-story building. Title in hand, I took Mom to see it.

We stood across the street from it for a few minutes, staring in happy disbelief at the blue, narrow, unadorned building that now belonged to us. It seemed lost on a busy commercial district. And yet, to me, it was a castle where my dreams were about to come true.

Mom had become quiet and still, as if she couldn't take another step. Turning toward her, I saw tears rolling down her cheeks. She took my hand and gripped it so tight that I had to say, "Mom, you're hurting me."

She let go of my hand, brushed the tears from her face with her fingers, and said in a low, quivering voice, "I think it's time for us to go back in."

I hooked my arm around hers, and we crossed the street, each step bringing us a little closer to the future. Each step leading me closer to understanding Leon's obsession with legacy. I had fixed my gaze on the entrance to what was once Grandpa's place when an unbidden thought hit me: *This is my legacy. It's in my blood. It's destiny.*

I unlocked the door and we walked into a deep, empty, spotless, white space. I watched Mom stand still in the middle of it, her head turning slowly from side to side. She said, "I don't remember it being this big."

"It's empty, that's why. It's waiting for us to fill it, bring it back to life."

Had she expected the place to be like it was when she was a child? I wished I could imagine how it had looked to her then. It had passed through several hands in the forty years since Grandma sold it. The owner I bought it from ran a sandwich shop.

I said, "It's ours again. To turn into a food mecca that makes people smile when they bite into your tarts or my matelote de poisson. Like they once did for Grandpa's dishes."

Mom nodded. "What are we waiting for, then?"

She had brought a framed picture she inherited from Grandma—Grandpa, in a chef's uniform, smiling and standing next to a refrigerated food case. Mom tore off its brown paper wrapping and took a hammer and nails out of her bag. I asked if she needed help. She shook her head.

She hung the picture, taking her time; her movements meditative as she measured, marked, drove nails into the wall, and adjusted the picture. It was as if she was performing a religious ritual.

Mom stood looking at the image of Grandpa. After some time, she turned to me and smiled, her eyes moist. I knew then that coming back to this place was what she needed to finally be at peace with her memories of one of the cruelest things that could happen to a child.

*****

I wasn't fully prepared to open and run a restaurant, or a French artisanal delicatessen like Grandpa's, but my family was eager to help. And Laure was generous with advice and information, sharing her sources for French products. She hooked me up with her trusted accountant who monitored our expenditures.

We resurrected Grandpa's recipes that my grandmother had stored in a locked box. Recipes written in a mix of English and French that she had to translate for us. From those recipes, Mom and I put together our first menu. I decided to put off inventing new dishes until we have attracted a steady clientele.

A little more than a year ago, I opened my own brand of eatery after months of planning and hard work.

On the street, passersby see a yellow orange awning jutting out on the sidewalk. Emblazoned on its front, in dark blue letters, is our tribute to Grandpa: *Chez Merleau,* after his last name.

That yellow awning is the touch the once-forlorn building needed for it to look like it belonged on the street. And during the first half of the day, customers coming in and out and the line that sometimes forms outside entice potential customers to come in and check us out.

When they enter, Grandpa greets them from his perch on the wall a couple of feet from the door.

Like Grandpa, I offer my versions of French classics—cassoulet, boeuf bourguignon, coq au vin, poulet basquaise, ratatouille, bouillabaisse. They're vacuum-sealed in bags that can be heated a few minutes in boiling water. They're popular enough that they sell out by late afternoon.

We also offer homemade patés that Mom makes; country hams and cheeses imported from France; and sweet and savory croissants, tartlets, and moelleux au chocolat that Mom, Sabine, Gerard, and I make together. Gerard's interest in baking surprised us, and Mom thinks he's a natural at it.

Though Chez Merleau is more a deli than a bistro, we have ten inside and outside tables for customers who eat *sur place*.

Every morning when I open for business, I remind myself that I owe what I now have to Leon. His generosity has helped me come a long way from where I was six years ago when running my own restaurant seemed an impossible dream.

*****

At a soft knock on my office door, I put down the bill from one of our suppliers that I've been checking. Rachel, one of two students who help with lunch hour rush, comes in and stands by the door. We met at the university when we were waiting in line to petition for a new section of a required class that filled quickly.

"Gina, there's a guy at the counter. Wants to talk to you."

"Come in, Rachel. Did he say who he is?"

"No. I didn't think to ask. A tall guy, thirtyish, dark suit, neatly-trimmed beard. He looks cool but a bit intimidating, like a lawyer, though I've never seen one with a beard. His does look good on him."

I laugh. "You're tingling."

She laughs, too. "Can't resist cute guys."

"I'd better go check him out then."

"More your type, actually."

"Then I'd be disappointed if all he wants is to place an order," I say, laughing again.

"I think he's in need of something else. Looks a bit tense. Anyway, I'm going now. Nell is still here."

"Yeah, she stays until Sabine comes. Thank you for helping today. We'll see you tomorrow. Use the back door. It's quicker."

"Okay, thanks. See you."

*****

From ten feet away, the man waiting at the counter looks vaguely familiar but he's back-lit and shadows obscure his face. I can swear, though, that I've seen that build in that tall frame before. My curiosity mounts as I approach him. It can't be, I murmur to myself. He'd never wear a suit like that, and his boss probably won't let him grow a beard.

I stare at the man, conscious of my heart beating faster. He's smiling, though he looks uneasy. A couple of steps closer, I see his eyes more clearly. And I stop. I grip the sides of my apron to steady myself. How could

I forget those deep-set gray eyes that couldn't look away from violence?

"Regine," he says, "how are you?"

The same voice from far away reverberates in my brain, anguished, quivering, and eventually fading away: *Regine, my love.*

I smile, cautiously, and I wonder: *Did you really call me "my love?"* I approach the counter, grateful it's there between us.

"Brent, as I live and breathe, resurrected from the abyss. In an impeccable dark suit." Somehow, I manage to sound casual.

He wiggles his lapel and looks embarrassed. "I can explain this if you join me for coffee and croissant."

"I'll sit with you, but I've just had lunch." I'm lying about lunch because my gut is roiling and would reject intrusions from my gullet.

Sitting on a high stool by the counter, Nell is gazing out at the street, trying in vain to look bored. Her eyes are shining and darting about with curiosity. She glances quickly at me but addresses Brent. "I'll bring your coffee and croissant to your table. What kind of croissant would you like?"

"A ham and cheese, if you have it," Brent says.

Nell flashes him a beguiling smile. "Yes, we do."

Amused, I arch an eyebrow at Nell and follow Brent to a table. He chooses one farthest away from other occupied tables.

"You're looking great," he says as soon as we sit down.

"How did you find me?"

"I worked as a detective, remember?"

"Worked?"

"I changed jobs a year ago."

"Where you have to wear a suit and tie?"

"I was at court today. I now work at the public defender's office."

We both look up as Nell approaches. She stands next to Brent as she unloads two cups of coffee, a plate of croissant, and a small carafe of milk on the table.

I say, "Thank you, Nell."

This time, it's she who arches an eyebrow at me. Nell doesn't know my history and like Rachel, she thinks I'm married to Chez Merleau. Occasionally, they tease me about setting me up with their older friends, brothers or cousins.

In a jaunty tone that compels Brent to look up at her, she says, "*Bon appetit*" with her sweetest smile. She throws me another glance and sashays back to the counter.

Brent's gaze follows her sashaying figure. I wait a few seconds before I hand him the milk. "So, you've decided to use your law degree. At the same office as that smart lawyer who got Cristi out of having to face trial?"

He pours milk into his coffee, takes a few sips, and pours a little more milk.

"Would you like some whipped cream on that?"

He smiles in the guarded way he had when we first met. "No, thank you. You remember. And yes. I decided to change my priorities, which I can tell you more about later. But as to how I found you—" He looks up from his coffee. "I was going to ask your mother, but before I could, Marcia called to ask if we could remain friends, and she told me about your French delicatessen."

"Marcia," I say bitterly. "She's out, then."

"No, but she may be released in a few months on good behavior. She's been evaluated by a psychologist and he doesn't think she's a danger to others or to herself. Plus she got herself a good lawyer. I won't be surprised if she tries to contact you later. She's in touch with Laure, who'll probably take her back."

"How kind and generous of Laure. But she won't tell Marcia where I am, so one of the cooks at Du Cœur must have blabbered to Marcia."

"Maybe. Anyway, she told me something else which concerns you."

"Me? I'd rather she doesn't concern herself about me anymore."

"I understand how you feel, but you should hear what she said. It's about Laure. And you."

I shrug. "Anything about Laure is interesting, and I sure want to know if it's about me."

"Laure was interviewed by the San Francisco Magazine for her recommendations of up and coming chefs. You're on her list of three."

Though I would have preferred the source of this news to be someone other than Marcia, I'm excited and incredulous, and couldn't help grinning, "No way! For real?"

People listen to Laure. Chez Merleau gets enough customers to break even, but an endorsement from her would surely attract more people and widen my customer base.

"For real." This time, Brent unleashes a bright, spontaneous smile.

My excitement doesn't last—Marcia is a palpable shadow that continues to haunt me. "But how did Marcia find out?"

"Maybe the same way she learned where you are."

I look away, shuddering. Marcia has obviously kept in touch with her friends, including Brent. Never again would I want to be one of them. She still spooks me, and I don't know if I can ever forgive her.

Brent reaches over to clasp my hand. "Regine. Gina, I'm still here."

I say, ignoring the plea I heard in his voice, "So, how's Marcia?"

"Does it bother you that I'm in contact with her?"

I don't answer. I pull my hand from his grasp, pick up my cup, and sip my coffee.

"She called me that morning, you know, as soon as she left you to tell me what she had done to you. An attack of conscience, I think. Guilt can be powerful. Marcia is a lonely, tragic woman who was so distraught over what she did that I felt I had to stay in touch with her through her trial."

"I don't want to talk about how she tried to kill me. It hurts too much. She was my best friend."

"I don't condone what she did to you. But she isn't bad at heart."

"That's what they all say. Including me when I excused Cristi for stabbing me. But it's much harder for me to say it about Marcia. I looked up to her, trusted her almost as much as I did my mother. How could she stalk me, send me threatening messages, and try to kill me."

"Marcia had a lot of pent-up anger. It's been building since she was jilted by the Oregon man she was engaged to. She dated Leon for a while, a relationship that lasted longer than most except yours. She saw you get everything she wanted, and the dam broke. The nicest people are capable of killing when pushed to their limits. And she had no one, Regine."

Brent must know what he's saying, and I can even believe Marcia is so needy that she gets victimized. But she's also capable of inflicting serious pain, and becoming the victimizer. *No, Brent, I'm not closer to forgiving her. And it doesn't help that you're trying to excuse what she did to me.*

I wanted to say "No one? She has you and those cooks at Du Cœur." But that sounds petulant, so I say wryly, "You're kinder than I am."

"No, not really. It's my conscience. I wonder if I might have used her, too. I hadn't known she was fragile until ..."

Sighing, I cut him off. I'm losing my patience. All I want now is to end all this talk about Marcia. "If you're talking about having sex with her, she knew what she was doing. She had designs on you before you got into her bed. That dinner we had, I set it up for her. She asked me to hook her up with you. "

Brent seems at a loss what to make of my disclosure. He says, "I see. Oh Regine... You know, there was never anything between us. It was over a couple of months after it began."

This is news to me. Marcia led me to believe their affair went on for months.

When I stay silent, Brent leans forward and clasps my hand again. "I started on the wrong foot today. I shouldn't have brought up Marcia. Will you give me a chance to redeem myself? Have dinner with me?"

"Is that why you came, to ask me to dinner? If so, you're right. Starting out defending Marcia didn't help."

"I'm truly sorry. My mind is so full of things I want to say to you, and I don't know exactly where or how to begin. I thought having dinner together would ease us back to the way we were before...."

I cut him off again. I just couldn't stand hearing Marcia's name again. "Well, then, let's go out to dinner. I think that's a good place to start."

Brent looks startled. I hope it's because he's surprised at how easy it would have been if he just asked me to dinner right away. He says, "All right."

I rise from my chair, tired and suddenly hungry. "Can you pick me up at seven? I know a Japanese restaurant where we don't need a reservation."

He gets up, but he seems reluctant to leave,

"We'll have all the time we could want to say what needs to be said. Just a few more hours," I say wearily.

He nods, squeezes my hand, and walks away slowly.

*****

We have dinner that evening at a Japanese izakaya. Like a tapas bar, it serves small plates with drinks. The place is buzzing—everyone is talking in excited voices fueled by bottles of sake. I don't mind the loud conversations, and Brent doesn't seem to, either. But am I putting off painful explanations by taking him to this place?

I pause before I spear a piece from the first dish we ordered—a plate of breaded fried shrimp coated in a sweet-sour sauce. Why did I bring Brent here, apart from the scrumptious food?

I think it's because of the bustle. It makes this place safe for our kind of reunion. After three years of being apart, I believe Brent and I need to just be together, and not feel compelled to talk. Like I told him earlier, we'll have all the time for explanations.

When I first saw him at my French deli this afternoon, standing by the counter, I froze and tasted acid shooting up from my gut. I was apprehensive. I couldn't tell at that instant how I felt about having him come back into my life. He'll change the new life I've just started to fashion for myself. Take me out of my current comfort zone. Am I ready for that?

I watched him as he walked away after I agreed to have dinner with him. He seemed hesitant to leave and I found myself thinking:. *Does this mean he still loves me? How could I not seize this moment? He's the one I've truly, deeply loved.*

I wasn't ready. Not yet. I need to know how I feel about having someone other than myself to please and live for. Something other than Chez Merleau to devote my time on.

Tonight, in this lively crowd, we can both keep any intense emotions at bay while we sit here just keeping company with each other amidst a group of strangers. Enjoying this meal. Talking when we could above the din of sake-soaked voices. Feeling what it's like to be together again. Maybe, as I get used to the idea that Brent is back in my life, I'll be able to cope better with whatever happens next.

We say very little on the way back to my home, a spacious apartment above Chez Merleau that came as part of the sale. He turns off the car engine in front of the building.

I vacillate about what to do. Say goodnight after a quick kiss, or ask Brent up to my apartment?

He senses my hesitation and says, "Wait." He gets out of the car and comes to my side. He opens the passenger door.

Nights are quiet in this largely business section of the city. Tourists and workers enliven the place in the daytime, and vacant parking spaces are hard to find. But at this time of night, the streets are quiet, devoid of people and cars. There's only Brent and me to disturb the tranquility.

The empty streets often fill me with loneliness and dread, but tonight, the stillness summons a sense of entering a dream. And in my dreams, everything happens the way I want them to.

Brent follows me wordlessly to my door and up the steps to my apartment. I'm aware he's making decisions for both of us, and I'm okay with it.

In the living area, I deposit my purse on the side table at one end of the couch. "Make yourself comfortable. Would you like a nightcap? I have some Grand Marnier, an orange liqueur."

"No, thank you. Let's just talk."

"Okay." I sit on the couch.

He takes an armchair facing me. A small rectangular coffee table separates us. He pushes the chair closer to the table and leans forward, clasping his hands. "There's so much I want to say to you, I don't know where to start."

"How about the thing that matters to you most, what you would say if you only had a second to say it."

He gazes into my eyes and says. "I still love you, Regine. I want to be a part of your life. And if you let me, you'll be the most important part in mine."

Surprised, I couldn't answer for some moments. Even when he told me he loved me at the Emeryville coffeehouse, he had said his work was his passion. One he couldn't let go of. I took it to mean he wouldn't give it up for a relationship.

"At the coffeehouse, you tried to dissuade me from marrying Leon by saying you loved me. And yet, you weren't ready for the kind of permanent relationship he was offering me. What has changed, Brent?"

"I loved you then as I love you now. But that time, I thought I was saving you from becoming one of Leon's victims. That if you and I confessed we loved each other, you wouldn't marry Leon. It was only later I realized I couldn't bear to see you marry him or any other man."

"But that would have been too late because I had already agreed to marry Leon."

"You're right. And I could only blame myself, regret it my whole life if that had happened. But sometimes, it takes some crisis for us to realize what we really want. And with some luck, we could do something to get what we desire most.

"Before we saw each other at the coffeehouse, Marcia had already told me stories about you and Leon. You had moved in with him. You looked happy. You said it was paradise living with Leon. He was a whiz in bed. Those stories have tortured me ever since. I know how beguiling and irresistible he could get. I also know his history with women. When she told me you were getting married, I felt I had to rescue you from him."

I suppress a smile—Brent, the compassionate rescuer, though I think his interference was misguided. And he did have self-interest.

I say, "I never said any of those things to Marcia. She asked many times about life with Leon, but I just shrugged her off. I said no one could match the passion you and she had together."

Brent groans. "Marcia is a provocateur. But thinking you and Leon were together wasn't my worst agony. When she called to tell me she made you swallow a bottle of sleeping pills, I rushed to your address. Lucky that I'd been carrying your keys in my pocket. The drive was hell. Even with the police siren on, I couldn't get to you fast enough. I saw you on the couch. So still, clutching a bottle you wouldn't let go of. It was then I realized I'd do anything so I don't lose you again. "

"Were you walking along the gurney when I was taken to the hospital?"

"I didn't want to leave your side until I was sure you were going to be okay."

"Did you visit me later?"

"I came every morning before going to work. And I came in the evening."

"Did you ever say 'Regine, my love'?"

"You heard me."

"I thought it was a dream. But why didn't you come and visit me when I regained consciousness?"

"Your mother requested I stay away for a while. She was protecting you. She said you needed time to recover among people who're familiar, who you knew loved you. It was too much, she said—first Cristi, then Marcia. There was also the breakup with Leon. She said, 'if you truly love her, you can wait. You'll come back, maybe in a year. I think you also have things to sort out.' She's wise, your mother."

"Is that why you went back to law?"

Brent smiles. "I decided I wanted to be with you every day of my life, and not only when you need me."

"Don't you miss your search for justice and truth?"

"No. I'm actually finding law more fulfilling, and definitely less stressful. I can look at the questions that have bothered me from different angles. Or eventually learn to accept that I'll never be able to answer them."

Brent gets up and sits next to me on the couch. He wraps my hands with his. "Can you love me again, my Regine?"

I don't answer, but as I gaze back at him, I see us again on that night when we first made love.

"Do you still love Leon?"

"I have Chez Merleau because of Leon. It will always remind me of him. He did love me, but I've wondered if he can love anyone as much as he loves himself. When he asked me to marry him, I had given up on you, and I had learned to love him enough to say yes. His father objected, threatened to disinherit him. Leon chose his legacy. He said it was his destiny."

Brent isn't satisfied with my response. "But do you still love him?"

"My love for Leon had a lot to do with gratitude. It was never anything like I've felt for you. You must know that."

"What you felt for me—is it too late for me to rekindle it?"

"Whatever drew us to each other in the beginning—do you think it dies that easily?"

"Not for me. No, it hasn't. That's why I'm here. Because I've finally admitted to myself that I can't be happy, that I can't feel whole without you."

Once again, words fail me. I can't quite believe everything that's happened today. Lately, I've wondered whether my experience with Leon has turned me off of relationships. Maybe, I've just been waiting for Brent. Somehow, I knew he'd come back to me.

Tears are beginning to blur my vision. Tears, neither of sadness nor of warring emotions, but of pure, utter happiness.

Brent gathers me in his arms. I lay my head on his shoulder. He whispers in my ear, "Oh my love. So much I have to make up for."

I want to tell him: I don't need any more explanations. What else is there to say? Aren't my tears of joy eloquent enough?

I don't want you to atone for your imagined sins, Brent. All I want is for you to love me. Intensely, sincerely like I know you know how.

He takes my hand, kisses it and lays it briefly on his chest. Like that night after the dinner in Marcia's apartment.

I raise my face to him. "Will you stay with me tonight?"

He kisses me. "Yes."

Liked what you read? Check out more of Evy's books and writing: Get this one free:

If you enjoy thoughtful prose that significantly touches the heart, this is definitely one of the best I've read.
Wanda Pile, Amazon Reviewer

Book Blurb: Five short stories. Five people. From Paris to Honolulu. At moments that matter most, each is all alone. But it's then that she has the clearest vision of herself.

Get this book for free: Sign up at Evy Writes: https://evyjourney.net/free-brief-encounters/.

More Books by Evy Journey

Between Two Worlds

A series of six standalone tales about negotiating separate, sometimes clashing, realities

Set 1

A family saga.
Three tales of loss, love, second chances, and finding one's way.
Laced with a twist of mystery, the healing power of music, and international political intrigue.

Hello, My Love (Book 1)

A modern-day pastiche of Jane Austen's Pride and Prejudice with a twist of whodunit.

Hello, Agnieszka (Book 2)

A seventies story of love, betrayal, and the healing power of music.

Welcome Reluctant Stranger (Book 3)

Can she run away from a mysterious past in the Pacific Island she was forced to flee as a child?

Set 2

Three multicultural, multiracial women.
Their passion for cooking, travel, and art.

And their adventures navigating an unfamiliar, sometimes menacing world.

Sugar and Spice and All Those Lies (Book 4)

Chanterelles garnished with cream and mayhem.

The Shade Under the Mango Tree (Book 5)

Can she emerge unscathed from a world steeped in ancient culture and the ravages of a deadly history. An award-winning tale.

The Golden Manuscripts: A Novel (Book 6)

In her quest for stolen art, she discovers a passion and a home.

Margaret of the North

Can a Victorian feminist tame her man? A North and South sequel.

Brief Encounters with Solitary Souls

"Life is for each man a solitary cell whose walls are mirrors"—Eugene O'Neill

About the Author

Evy Journey is a writer, a wannabe artist, and a flâneuse. Her pretensions to being a flâneuse means she wishes she lives in Paris where people have perfected the art of aimless roaming.

She's a writer because beautiful prose seduces her and existential angst continues to plague her despite such preoccupations having gone out of fashion. She takes occasional refuge by invoking the spirit of Jane Austen and spinning tales of love, loss, and finding one's way. Stories set in various locales into which she weaves mystery or intrigue.

In a previous life, fascinated by the psyche and armed with a Ph.D., she researched and shepherded the development of mental health programs. Now, she writes mostly happy fiction.

Connect with the author:

Website: Evy Writes: https://evyjourney.net

Book review blog:

Escape Into Reality:

https://margaretofthenorth.wordpress.com

Musings on art, travel, food:

Artsy Rambler: https://eveonalimb2.com

Facebook Page:

https://www.facebook.com/ejourneywriter/